Joseph

JAMES R. SHOTT

HERALD PRESS
Scottdale, Pennsylvania
Waterloo, Ontario

Library of Congress Cataloging-in-Publication Data
Shott, James R., 1925-
Joseph / James R. Shott
p. cm.
ISBN 0-8361-3576-8
1. Joseph (Son of Jacob)—Fiction. 2. Bible. O.T.—History of Biblical events—Fiction. I. Title.
PS3569.H598J67 1991
813'.54—dc20 91-32866
CIP

The paper used in this publication is recycled and meets the minimum requirements of American National Standard for Information Sciences—Permanence of Paper for Printed Library Materials, ANSI Z39.48-1984.

JOSEPH
Copyright © 1992 by Herald Press, Scottdale, Pa. 15683
Published simultaneously in Canada by Herald Press, Waterloo, Ont. N2L 6H7. All rights reserved.
Library of Congress Catalog Number: 91-32866
International Standard Book Number: 0-8361-3576-8
Printed in the United States of America
Book design by Paula M. Johnson/Cover art by Mary Chambers

1 2 3 4 5 6 7 8 9 10 97 96 95 94 93 92

To Esther,
who has enriched my life with love,
companionship, guidance, and joy
for more than forty-three years.
I'm looking forward to at least
forty-three more!

1

"Let's kill him!"

The savage words burst from the lips of one of three men standing on Dothan hill with their backs to the late afternoon sun. Their travel-stained robes and shepherd staffs proclaimed their occupation. Dust and sweat tangled their short dark beards. They stared into the east, watching the solitary figure in the distance walk toward them.

One turned and spoke to the man who had uttered the violent words. "Simeon," he said. "If you kill Joseph, you'll probably kill Father, too."

Simeon spun around and glared at his accuser. "You're too soft, Reuben," he growled. "That rotten dreamer deserves to die. If it were up to me, I'd carve him up with my blade."

"He's our brother, Simeon." Reuben's voice reflected the patience of the mature elder brother. "We share the same father."

"He's no brother of mine." Simeon's lips curled. "He's Rachel's son. He's not one of *us*."

Now Reuben hardened his tone. "I promised our mother Leah that no harm would come to him. I mean to keep that promise."

"Would you protect that stinking piece of sheep's dung? Remember the stories he told Father about us? Remember the dreams he boasted about, where we bow down before him? You know he looks down on us, flaunting his favoritism. He deserves to die!"

Through this exchange the third man had said nothing. He gazed steadily from under the hand shading his eyes at the approaching figure. Now he spoke, pointing toward the boy in the distance.

"Look, brothers! He wears his gilded robe."

The other men gazed in the direction of his pointing finger. The late afternoon sun glistened on the gold filigree adorning the long purple robe. A gust of desert wind picked up the long sleeves. They ballooned haughtily.

Reuben shifted uncomfortably. "What do you make of it, Judah? He wears his dainty dress even out here in the desert."

Simeon spat on the ground. "He's throwing it in our faces," he muttered. "He's reminding us he's our father's favorite, that filthy son of a diseased pig!"

"I hope he has no more dreams to tell us," said Judah. "Our brothers are still boiling over the last one."

"If he tells us another dream," said Simeon savagely, "I'll kill him! I don't care what it does to Father. Levi will help. So will all the others. What do you say, Judah?"

Reuben spoke angrily. "No! If you want to teach him a lesson, put him in that empty cistern on the other side of Dothan hill. Just for a day or two. Let him think it over. But no killing! I'm still the oldest, and I forbid it!"

Judah pulled his short beard, his swarthy forehead creased with a deep frown.

"Why kill him? That Ishmaelite trader encamped on the other side of Dothan hill might buy him from us. Let's sell him into Egyptian slavery."

"Slavery or killing, it's all the same to me," said Simeon, still glowering. "Just so we silence his dreams and his tattling forever."

Reuben turned on his brother, his beard thrust out. Ordinarily a soft-spoken person, he now spoke with fire. "There'll be neither murder nor slavery! I—"

Simeon's lips curled. "You're as soft as a sheep's coat in winter," he snarled. "And your memory is as short as its summer coat. Have you forgotten that he was the one who told Father about your seducing his concubine? You could have lost your birthright, and it would have been his fault!"

Reuben's body tensed. His face turned red under his tan, accenting his black beard. He seemed about to say something, but instead he turned abruptly and walked down the hill toward his incoming younger brother.

Simeon laughed caustically. "Now that he's gone, Judah, let's get down to business. Shall we kill him, or shall we sell him to the Ishmaelite?"

"Let's not kill him," Judah spoke thoughtfully. "We can get thirty pieces of silver for him. But I'm still not sure we should do that. What would Father think if we did this to his favorite son?"

Simeon smiled, although his frown made his smile look malevolent. "We can tell Father a wild animal killed him. We can tear his pretty robe and dip it in goat's blood. Let him grieve awhile. He'll get over it."

"But we can't do it while Reuben is here. We have no quarrel with him."

"Then let's do it tonight, while Reuben is taking his watch with the flock. Reuben just gave us a good way to do it. We'll put Joseph in that dry well between our camp and the Ishmaelite's. Then in the morning we'll make a deal with the traders and be rid of the foppish dreamer forever."

Judah's eyes narrowed as he turned to watch his brother Reuben, who had reached the foot of Dothan hill and was walking rapidly toward Joseph. "All right," he said, nodding slowly. "But the quicker we do it, the better. You talk to our brothers and arrange for Joseph to be taken to the pit tonight while Reuben is out with the sheep. I'll go to the Ishmaelite and see if he would be willing to take him away before dawn."

"Good! It's about time we do something." Simeon turned to go.

Judah remained for a moment rooted to the hillside, gazing at his older brother's back, slowly shaking his head. Finally he shrugged, then turned and walked slowly toward the Ishmaelite's camp.

When Reuben came up to Joseph, his greeting was cool. "Joseph," he said curtly. "What brings you here? And why are you showing off that robe?"

"Greetings, brother." Joseph's grin set off his handsome face. At seventeen, he was without a beard. His soft brown eyes met Reuben's with a self-assurance bordering on impudence. "One thing at a time. Now, about why I'm here. Father sent me to find out how things are going. I missed you at Shechem, so I came here."

Reuben frowned. "In your pretty robe? You shouldn't wear that kind of dress in the wilderness."

"Don't worry, Reuben. Nothing can happen to me. I'm under God's protection!"

Reuben clenched his fist, then took a deep breath. "Joseph, you mustn't talk like that. Don't you know what it does to your brothers? They think you look down on them."

"Let them think what they like; I don't care. They don't like me very much, do they?"

The two began to walk toward the brothers' camp at the foot of Dothan hill. They made quite a contrast: one shaggy, bearded, and dirty, his short burnoose tattered and stained; the other young and fresh and gleaming in his long regal garment.

"I'd better warn you about your brothers, Joseph.

They'll kill you if you continue to flaunt Father's favoritism so openly."

Joseph smiled benignly. "I'm telling you, Reuben, no harm will come to me. God has great things planned for my future. I'm sure of it. I've had another dream."

Reuben sighed. "Another dream! Your last one was bad enough. I don't think I want to hear about this one."

Joseph laughed. "I'll tell you anyway. There was one star in the sky brighter than anything else. All the other stars bowed before it. Even the moon and sun bowed low."

Reuben stopped, grasped his brother's shoulder and spun him around facing him. "Whatever you do, don't tell your brothers about this. They'll kill you on the spot!"

"Aw, don't worry, Reuben. They won't hurt me." Joseph lifted his chin. "I have a destiny!"

"Joseph, stop! You're going too far!" Reuben's spoke through clenched teeth. "You're tempting disaster. Be careful!"

"If you say so, Reuben." The words were agreeable, but Joseph's attitude belied his words.

A few minutes later they marched into camp. The eight men there busied themselves with small camp-tasks and avoided looking at Joseph. Simeon turned his back and walked over to the camels.

Joseph seemed not to notice his brothers' coolness. He lifted his voice. "Come, brothers, let's relax and have some fun. I have traveled far today looking for you. You've been gone a long time, and Father is anxious about you. He thinks you're in Shechem. What will he say when I have to tell him you're in Dothan?"

No one spoke. Nobody looked at him. Joseph ignored this and blundered on. "What's in the cooking pot, Levi? It smells like a kid. I hope it's young and tender, in honor of my coming."

Levi frowned, his short black beard thrust forward.

"You'll wait your turn," he growled. "Don't forget, you *are* the youngest."

Joseph said nothing but grinned as though he knew something the others didn't.

Reuben stepped forward and spoke curtly. "Let's eat," he said. He ladled some stew into a bowl and walked to the edge of the camp to sit and eat. The brothers followed him. They ate in silence, avoiding any further contact with Joseph.

Reuben finished first. "I have the middle watch," he muttered. He shot a warning glance at Joseph as he wrapped his burnoose around him and lay down by the fire.

"Good night, brother," said Joseph cheerfully. "I hope your dreams are as pleasant as mine."

Reuben sat up suddenly and looked around. There was a cold silence. Nobody moved. Nobody spoke. Then suddenly the tense moment was over, as the brothers turned away and silently continued eating.

Reuben glared sternly at Joseph, trying to communicate wordlessly his warning. Joseph only grinned impudently, and Reuben eased himself down and closed his eyes.

The night wore on; the camp was unusually quiet. Joseph tried to start a conversation, but the brothers ignored him. Finally he shrugged his shoulders, yawned, and sat down near the fire. He wrapped his long robe around him several times, thankful for its plentiful material since it was thinner than the coarse wool his brothers wore. He then settled himself beside Reuben and was soon asleep.

He awakened in the night and sat up, startled. Something was wrong. Reuben had gone, probably to take his watch with the sheep. Joseph glanced around, noticing darting figures in the semidarkness. He shuddered.

It happened quickly. Powerful hands seized Joseph from behind. A rough hand was clapped over his mouth.

He struggled, but the hands that held him were strong. Someone bound his arms behind him and wrapped a dirty sash around his head. His scream was muffled in heavy folds.

He could not see through the sash that bound his face, but he could hear clearly the sounds of activity in the camp. Simeon's voice blared out.

"Let's kill him. Right now! I'll do it myself. My blade thirsts for his blood!"

Judah's voice thundered with a newfound authority. "Put that away, Simeon. We agreed not to kill him. Bring him along."

Rough hands grasped Joseph's arms, half dragging, half pushing. He stumbled between them, keeping on his feet only because they held his arms. His robe left behind, he wore only a loincloth. The chill night air prickled his skin.

He stumbled along for a while, shivering equally from fear and the cold wind. Then he was jerked to a stop. Judah's voice gave the orders.

"Let him down easy. Don't hurt him. It'll damage his value."

Someone kicked Joseph's feet from under him, and he was shoved slowly into a hole. They lowered him, held by his armpits, and then dropped. He landed feet first and crumpled onto the floor of the pit.

Then, silence. Deep, empty silence. There was nothing left but the dark, cold, and the creeping terror. He was alone in the empty darkness.

2

The sudden silence shook Joseph. He was alone, his brothers gone, and the relentless darkness enveloped him. In the vacuum of sound, he began to hear little noises one by one, little animals creeping around on the floor of the cistern. Snakes? Spiders? Scorpions?

Something ran across Joseph's bare foot. He jerked his leg up to his body. He shuddered, close to panic.

Get hold of yourself, he thought. He struggled to sit up, his hands tied behind his back making it difficult. *You're all right. God is with you. Remember your dreams.*

This brought him a little peace. Nothing could happen to him. He was under God's protection. God had great things in mind for him; he wouldn't die in this awful pit.

The sash around his head was making breathing hard. Leaning over, he rubbed his face on the ground until the sash finally slid down around his neck. He took in deep gulps of air.

Again something ran over his foot, but he had control of himself now. He grinned. *No snake or scorpion will dare bite me. God will not permit it. Not me. I am God's chosen.*

His brothers would pay. God would punish them. Just wait. Nothing—nobody—could interfere with his destiny. They'd pay. Pay dearly.

"Joseph!"

The voice sounded far above him. Reuben! God had

sent him! He grinned in the darkness.

"I'm down here, brother."

"Joseph, are you all right? Are you hurt?" Reuben's voice was concerned.

"I'm fine, Reuben. Just get me out."

There was a moment's silence, then Reuben's voice above him spoke firmly. "No, Joseph. I can't. Our brothers would just find you and put you back in. You'll have to stay down there for a while."

Joseph's self-assurance wavered. The familiar stab of fear churned in his stomach.

"Reuben, please. Don't leave me! You've got to do something!"

Another pause. Joseph clenched his teeth. "Are you there?"

"I'm here. But I must leave if I'm going to help you."

"Leave? You'll leave me? Don't, Reuben! You can't leave me now!"

"Be patient, Joseph. I can't help you. Only our father can control our brothers. I'll have to go to him and bring him here."

"Take me with you, Reuben!"

"No, Joseph. You must stay here. I'll take a donkey and ride to Hebron. Be there in the morning. I can have Jacob back here by evening."

"Will that be time enough? What if my brothers kill me in the morning?"

"Don't worry, Joseph. They won't kill you. They plan to sell you to the Ishmaelite for Egyptian slavery. But the Ishmaelite won't leave for two more days. He's waiting for the Midianites to join him. You'll be safe until then."

"Reuben, are you sure?"

"I'm sure." Reuben paused for a moment. "But Joseph, there's something else. How do we know this won't happen again?"

"What do you mean?"

"There will be another time, another place. Our brothers hate you. Father can't protect you forever."

"God will protect me, Reuben.

"You are arrogant, Joseph. You flaunt your favoritism and boast about your destiny. Can't you see why your brothers hate you? You're so smug. So superior."

"But Reuben—"

"Joseph, we don't have time to argue. Listen. You must promise you'll change your attitude toward your brothers. Don't look down on them and treat them like dirt. Act like a *younger* brother. Do you understand?"

Joseph sighed. "I suppose so."

"Think about it." The voice above him was steady. "And now I must go. Remember what I said."

"I'll remember. Please hurry."

"Good-bye, brother."

"Good-bye, Reuben."

Again the silence flooded down into the empty well, filling the cavern with its oppressing stillness. The little sounds of crawling things once more thrust themselves into Joseph's consciousness. Again the creeping terror, the inclination to panic. Joseph breathed slowly and deeply, and tried to think about God.

You are with me, God. I know you are. You have come to me in dreams. I have a destiny.

Don't I, God?

But the pit was empty. He was alone, except for the unseen crawling creatures. Where was God?

"God."

Joseph spoke the word aloud. Softly. But it sounded loud in the emptiness. The word had a cavernous, hollow ring.

"God."

Again he spoke into the emptiness. Again, nothing

there. Joseph shivered. He was naked except for his loincloth. The night air was chilly. It was the emptiness, the utter aloneness of the moment.

"God!" The words wrenched out of him in despair. "Where are you?"

His courage broke. The panic he had been warding off swept over him. He shuddered. Sobs shook his body. The terror of the night closed in upon him.

"Oh God! Where are you?" he shrieked.

He had no idea how long he sat in the darkness, sobbing and shuddering. His cries went into a void. He tried to think of his dreams, destiny, protection under God's power.

Nothing worked. He was alone. His terror was colder inside of him than the night air outside. The minutes dragged on, and sobs continued to convulse his body.

The hours lumbered by. By the time he heard voices above him, he was barely aware of them. Through a mist he heard his brother Judah's voice.

"He's down there, Son of Midian. He's yours, if you pay us thirty pieces of silver."

Joseph's mind was so deadened by terror he failed to grasp the significance of the title "Son of Midian." Later he would look back on that misty moment and realize what it meant. Reuben had said the Ishmaelite would not leave until the Midianites joined him. The Midianite was there.

"He is not worth thirty pieces of silver." The voice was gruff and heavily accented.

"Of course he is," said Judah. "He's young and healthy and intelligent. Thirty pieces of silver is the standard price for a slave."

"I pay no more than half price. Fifteen pieces of silver."

"But why?"

"Because of the risk. I'm afraid of Jacob. We know his reputation. He send bad army to kill us and get back son."

"But that has been arranged. Jacob won't know."

"You mistaken, Judah. Right now, your brother Reuben rides to Hebron to bring Jacob back. I pass him one hour ago on road. He ride fast donkey."

"Then you must take the boy and leave immediately."

"But how I know Jacob not follow?"

"We'll dip the boy's robe in goat's blood and show it to our father. He'll think a wild animal killed him."

The harsh voice in the darkness was silent a moment. "Let it be done. We accept the risk. But not for thirty pieces of silver. Risk worth half that price."

"We'll take five off. You may have him for twenty-five."

"Twenty."

"Agreed."

Joseph heard all this in a dreamlike trance. Then he began to hear the cold clink of silver being counted out, along with the hoarse voice of the trader mouthing the numbers. ". . . three, four, five. . . ."

Joseph's numbed mind could barely grasp what was happening. ". . . eight, nine, ten. . . ." That was his life, being counted out above him. That was the price of his destiny. He had been bargained over and discounted. He wasn't even worth the full price of a slave.

". . . thirteen, fourteen, fifteen. . . ." The raspy voice droned on. To Joseph's drugged mind it seemed to take forever. Was this how God protected him? Was this the destiny promised in his dreams? *Where are you, God?*

". . . twenty." The counting and clinking stopped. And with it Joseph's hope crashed. It was over. The end. He was a slave. No longer God's chosen. Nothing. Dead.

He was scarcely aware of the man who came down a rope into the pit. He tied the rope roughly around Joseph's chest. At his command, Joseph was rudely hoisted out. In a few minutes the boy was stumbling along behind a man who held the rope, leading him to a dismal destiny.

3

The Avenue of the Horses fascinated Joseph. The wide street embraced by statues and temples was a marvel to the untraveled boy from the hill country of Canaan. Accustomed to tents, he saw here immense, solid-looking buildings made of stone. Everything was clean and gleaming. Avaris, the capital city of upper Egypt, overwhelmed him.

He had just been sold to an Egyptian. The man who bought him was a middle-aged pudgy man with an impassive face. His new master had refused to put a slave collar on him.

Joseph now walked behind the master's chair along the Avenue of the Horses. Behind him marched a small escort of soldiers, attesting to the affluence of the great man seated in the chair.

But the chair! Joseph had never imagined anything like it. Supported on two long poles, held by twelve slaves, the conveyance could go anywhere the slaves could walk, and the great man who occupied it would never have to set foot on the ground until he arrived. Joseph saw several other chairs on the Avenue of the Horses, but none looked as elegant as his master's.

One of the slaves carrying the chair had a coughing problem. He struggled to keep pace with the others but could not stop his hackings. The other slaves glanced at him anxiously, fearful that a sudden spasm would upset the rhythm of their carrying.

And that's how it happened, without warning. The slave erupted with a spasm of coughing that nearly upset the chair. Only the strength of the men before and behind him prevented it from being tipped over. But the lurch caused the master to tense and grasp the arms of his chair.

Joseph acted without thinking. He stepped forward and reached for the pole at the place where the coughing man stood. He could not speak their language, but his action spoke eloquently. The coughing man shot him a grateful glance, then took Joseph's place behind the chair. The procession continued.

No one had objected to Joseph's rash act. Joseph wondered about that. But he had not seen the reaction of the man in the chair. The man had watched Joseph leap into the slave's place. He had noticed that one of the guards in the escort stepped forward, intending to shove Joseph back in place. A discreet shake of the master's head had sent the guard back in line.

Joseph quickly mastered the rhythm of carrying the chair. It was simply a matter of keeping in step with the man in front of him. After a few minutes he could do it easily, and his concentration was drawn again to the city around him.

Many different kinds of people roamed the streets of this cosmopolitan city of Avaris. They were all colors, from pale anemic-looking men to jet-black powerful Nubians. Mostly the people were clean shaven, both on head and face. Joseph guessed the bearded ones were foreigners. Egyptians obviously did not like hair.

Some of the people he saw wore slave collars. Many looked sullen and withdrawn, as though the lack of freedom had turned them in on themselves. Joseph determined not to let the blackness and despair of slavery destroy him, as it almost had at the beginning of his captivity. In the past month since his brothers' betrayal, he had struggled against despair. He had won—and had promised himself never to lose the struggle. The sight of the disgruntled slaves on the street reinforced his decision.

He wondered about his master, who would not allow a collar to be worn by his newly bought slave. In fact, the other slaves in the small entourage of this household wore no collars. The man in the chair must be a compassionate master. The thought brought Joseph a sense of relief. He would do his best to serve him.

Suddenly his attention was jerked to a sight so startling that he almost faltered in his rhythmic walk. A woman! Obviously from a well-to-do household, she walked along the side of the street with an escort of young men. But her clothes! She wore a gauzy linen robe hanging on her body so that her breast was bared. The dress was so flimsy he could see the outline of her body beneath it. Her open face under a blue wig showed no embarrassment, as though she had done this all her life.

Joseph sucked in his breath. Where he lived, women were almost completely covered from head to toe, with only the face showing. Modesty was a way of life, and nudity was reserved for intimate love situations. He jerked his eyes away and concentrated on his job.

It was well he did, because the entourage was turning. Joseph, on the outside pole, lengthened his stride to keep pace with the others in his line, while the bearers of the inside pole shortened their steps. They were leaving the Avenue of the Horses and going down a smaller side street which led to the Great River. They passed several solid-looking houses along the street. A residential district for the affluent, he surmised. Avaris evidently had its wealthy section. Did it also have a slum area?

They came to a large estate by the river, surrounded by

a wall decorated with designs in two shades of brown. Joseph studied the gate opening. It was made of a large stone arch delicately carved and painted with figures of people and manlike gods. As they turned into this gateway, Joseph gasped. He stared at an enormous palace, the likes of which he had never imagined existed.

The house was a dazzling white, with a stony solidarity combined with delicate grace. Only one story, it sprawled along the Great River, broken by rooms jutting out into the courtyard. Yet it was well-integrated and looked well-planned and carefully laid out. The total effect was beauty and simple elegance.

The caravan halted in the courtyard. At a word from the master, the slave who had recovered from his coughing spell stepped forward and took Joseph's place, giving him a grateful smile as he passed. Joseph first wondered why he had been replaced. But he understood as he watched the slaves skillfully accomplish the tricky maneuver of putting the chair down without tipping the master out.

A servant came out of the house and bowed before the master. Joseph judged him to be at least sixty, almost doddering in his arthritic clumsiness, his bony shoulders showing wrinkles and age spots. His bald head looked natural, not shaved like most Egyptians. He wore a loose linen garment slung over one shoulder.

Judging from the glances in his direction, the master and servant began talking about Joseph. Then the old servant stepped forward and beckoned Joseph to follow. They went into the house.

The first room looked more like a hall. They passed through it and out into another courtyard, this one opening to the river. The broad expanse of the Great River was a shimmering blue, cool and inviting in the heat of the day. A stone landing led down into the water.

The old servant handed Joseph a small round piece of

soft material and pointed toward the water, making a few rubbing motions on his body. Joseph smiled, then walked out on the ramp and stepped into the water. He took a few steps down, then the ramp leveled off to a platform with the water about waist high. He removed his loincloth and began to wash.

He turned his back to the house and faced the river while he lathered his body. Then a tap on the shoulder startled him. Whirling, he found himself staring into the shy face of a young girl about his age. She was clothed in a loose-fitting gauzy dress similar to the one he had seen on the street.

Joseph caught his breath. He stood waist deep in the water, stark naked before this partially nude girl. He could feel the warm flush on his face spread down his shoulders.

The girl giggled at Joseph's discomfort. Nudity evidently meant nothing to her. Raised in that warm climate, she had probably been naked in the presence of men all her life. They wore clothes for style, he decided, not modesty.

She reached for Joseph's tattered loincloth, and he numbly handed it to her. Then she turned and walked back into the house. Joseph hurriedly finished his bathing.

As he came out of the water, the same girl came out of the house walking toward him with a clean linen garment. There was no place to hide, so Joseph had to come to her and take the piece of cloth from her hand. He quickly put it on. The girl had called it a *schenti*, a combination loincloth and skirt which fit comfortably around his waist and tied conveniently. He was at least covered from waist to knees.

He glanced up from dressing to find that the girl had gone back into the house. The aged servant was coming out. Behind him, two slaves carried a large chair. They put the chair down in the center of the courtyard just as the master strode out of the house.

Two men accompanied him. One, a competent-looking

bald man in his early forties, carried a writing board, parchment, and pens. Obviously a scribe of some sort. He settled himself cross-legged on the ground and prepared to take notes.

The other man was a slave. He was bearded, dirty, and sweat-stained, evidently brought in from the field for this meeting. It occurred to Joseph that the slave was a Canaanite who would act as a translator.

The master seated himself comfortably on the chair. With the exception of the scribe, everyone else stood.

The bearded slave spoke in a heavy accent, reminding Joseph of the Ishmaelite trader. "The master has questions for you."

Joseph grinned. It was a welcome relief to be able to talk to somebody in this strange land. He rushed into several questions. "Where are you from? What's the master's name? Is this his house? Are you. . . ."

The bearded slave's mouth dropped open and his eyes widened. He raised his hand and spoke furtively. "Don't talk. Just answer questions." He then turned quickly to the master and a conversation in Egyptian followed.

The slave turned back to Joseph. "He wants to know your name and family."

Joseph smiled. "I am Joseph, son of Jacob who is called Israel. My grandfather was Isaac. My great-grandfather was Abraham. We are descendants of Terah, the patriarch of the land of Ur in the Chaldees."

The slave spoke in Egyptian, slowly repeating the names for the benefit of the scribe. Then at a word from the master, he turned to Joseph. "How did you come to be a slave?"

Joseph paused. How much should he tell? He decided on complete honesty, no matter what the consequences.

"We are a family of shepherds in the land of Canaan. I was my father's favorite, and my ten older brothers were jealous of me. They had a right to be."

Joseph dropped his eyes for a moment, then looked squarely at the master. "I had been arrogant and rude to them. They became angry and sold me to an Ishmaelite trader for Egyptian slavery. It's no more than I deserve."

This was translated immediately and volubly, and Joseph was aware of the master's keen gaze upon him. Then another question passed through the interpreter. "And how do you feel about slavery now?"

"It is God's will. I have accepted my lot in life. I am content." These few words, spoken easily now, reflected the inner struggle Joseph had had with himself during the past month. It wasn't until he had been able to say this to himself that he found peace.

The next question startled him. "Tell me about your God."

Joseph considered this. Again, how much should he say? He decided on brevity. "Our God has no name nor form that you can see. He spoke to our ancestor Abraham and called him out of the Chaldees and led him to Canaan. He has been our family God ever since. He is kind and loving, and cares for individuals."

After a translation pause came an even more surprising question. "And is your God with you now?"

Joseph had asked himself this question many times in the past month. He had been so sure of God's presence before he became a slave. The shattering experience of a night in the pit near Dothan hill had shaken his faith to its roots.

It wasn't just his brothers' betrayal and the life of servitude facing him. The certainty of God's presence had been superseded by a haunting and disturbing question in his mind, the same question his master asked now.

Throughout the weeks of captivity, he had pleaded with God again and again to give him that old assurance that

God's gentle hand was still upon him. But God was as absent from him as he had been in the Dothan pit.

When he spoke, his voice faltered. "I'm not sure. I . . . hope so."

Something of Joseph's inner turmoil must have communicated itself to the master as he looked intently at Joseph's face. Joseph wondered what he was thinking. The face was impassive. Yet Joseph suspected his master was a kindly man, so he ventured a question of his own.

"Is it permitted to ask the master a question?"

The slave gaped in amazement. He shook his head slightly, then turned to the master and translated Joseph's question. The master nodded.

"May I know my master's name and family?" He spoke respectfully and shyly.

The question was translated. The master's face softened. He even ventured a small smile. "Potiphar." He spoke the name directly to Joseph. Then he turned to his slave and spoke.

The slave translated. "Our master is Potiphar, a civil servant in the court of Pharaoh. He is married to Nefermati, and they have no children."

Joseph smiled. "Thank you. Now, how may I serve my master?"

Potiphar was visibly impressed when this was translated. He turned to the scribe and spoke briefly to him. The scribe nodded.

Then Potiphar turned to Joseph. Through the interpreter he said, "You will be assigned to assist my scribe. He will teach you our language and, if you prove adept, to read and write. Serve me well, Joseph, and you will not regret it."

"Thank you, sir. I shall."

The interview completed, Potiphar rose and went into the house, the others following. But more surprises were to come. The old servant came out to Joseph, followed by the young girl who carried some strange implements. Potiphar's chair was replaced by a low stool. The servant pointed to it. Joseph sat.

The girl stepped forward. With some shears and a razor, she began to shave his head and the face which was just beginning to sprout the first seedlings of a beard. Joseph knew by then that the Egyptians disliked hair. Just the opposite with his people, to whom a lot of hair on the head and face was a sign of manhood. But he was in Egypt now. He had to accept the fact that hair was ugly.

He smiled grimly as the girl worked on his balding head. Changes. Radical changes in his life. So he was to be an assistant to a scribe. And bald. He would serve a kindly master. And wear very few clothes and be in the presence of women who also wore very few clothes.

Help me, God. I'm going to need it.

4

Joseph sat cross-legged in the scribe's room, reading the last of several reports on Potiphar's wealth. Inventory time came once a year; he had compiled on parchment an immense listing of his master's assets.

Besides the river palace in Thebes, Potiphar owned two country estates, a fine stable of horses, and much livestock. His fields and orchards and barns produced most of what was consumed in the vast household. This last report listed all the slaves, which Joseph had broken down to household servants, skilled workmen, guards, and field hands. He carefully checked the list, then laid it aside.

By now he had grown accustomed to Potiphar's wealth. Seven years had flown by since the master had purchased him from the slave market. Joseph shook his head as he recalled his own personal prosperity during that brief time.

He had begun as a lowly scribe's assistant who didn't even know the language. As soon as he had mastered that, he was given instruction in writing. In two years he had learned the relatively easy hieratic script, which followed phonetically the sounds of the language. He had also mastered the difficult hieroglyphic writings, the picture script of classical documents and monuments.

Ordinarily a scribe would spend several years in the Great School of Scribes, learning not only the two kinds of writing, but also mathematics, bookkeeping, administrative procedure, and architectural engineering. Joseph, blessed with a good teacher, had risen to Master Scribe in two years.

Potiphar had then made Joseph assistant to the Chief Steward, the old man Joseph had met on his first day in Potiphar's house. Suti-met was a capable steward, whose outstanding quality was his ability to command people. He used Joseph's skills wisely, and Joseph assumed more and more responsibilities over the years.

As Suti-met aged, he became senile and his concentration faltered. Joseph took more initiative. Within two years he had become the virtual manager of Potiphar's household. When the old man had died three years before, Potiphar had appointed Joseph Chief Steward.

He rose from his cramped position on the floor and walked outside. The sun shimmered on the pastel blue waters of the Great River. A cooling breeze riffled through the palm trees. The inventory finished, Joseph could relax.

He looked across the yard to the small villa where he himself lived. Potiphar had thought so much of him that he had assigned the comfortable house and servants to Joseph when Suti-met died. It was a pleasant place to live, the servants having been well trained by the capable former Chief Steward. Each day Joseph walked the hundred yards up the grassy slope to the office in the main house.

How wonderfully God had blessed him! It was characteristic of Joseph that he gave God the credit for his personal prosperity in captivity. He was not the same arrogant youth he had been back in Canaan. It never occurred to him to accept what everyone else in the household believed, that his intelligence, industry, and pleasing personality, combined with Potiphar's indulgence of his favorite slave, was the cause of his success. To Joseph's mind, all the credit went to God.

His mind reached back over the years to those secure

feelings of his childhood, when he was so certain that God's presence was with him, and God's hand was leading him to a glorious destiny.

He smiled. Those old feelings of assurance had gradually come back through the years. Everything he had set his mind to had succeeded marvelously. Potiphar's house had increased its wealth and well-being since he had been placed in positions of authority. It was exciting!

He recalled Potiphar's piercing question to him only seven years ago. "Is your God with you now?"

Joseph's faltering answer was at least an honest one. "I don't know. I hope so." How different his answer would be today!

He had grown to love his master. Potiphar was the Pharaoh's chief executioner but was ill-suited for the job. Sensitive, he was sickened every time he had to put someone to death. He was as lenient and kind as his job allowed. And Joseph loved him for that.

Joseph loved Potiphar for another reason. He had heard the story of Potiphar's first marriage about twenty years ago, when his first wife died agonizingly while giving birth to a stillborn son. His heart went out to Potiphar. This might explain his master's unnatural interest in him. Perhaps in Potiphar's mind, Joseph had taken the place of his dead son.

Potiphar had remarried and his second wife, Nefermati, was a beauty. Joseph felt uncomfortable in her presence. There was always in her manner an unspoken invitation, a subtle nuance which suggested a much deeper relationship than just mistress and slave. He tried to avoid her, but in the past few years his position had forced him to be with her often. He tried always to treat her formally.

"Ah, there you are, Joseph!"

It was as though his thinking about her had conjured up her presence. He turned as she approached from the house. "Nefermati" meant "beautiful child." Her name was appropriate. As an adult, she was stunning.

Tall, thin, and graceful, she carried well her twenty-five years. Joseph did not know if she had hair, because she always wore a concealing wig with a grease cone on top. During the hot afternoon the perfumed fat in the cone would melt and drip down over her face and body, giving a glossy sheen to her smooth skin.

She wore the clean white linen *kalasaris* that revealed so much of her body. Joseph had long ago developed the habit of not looking at her directly. Even now, he turned his eyes away, so that he would not see the body she so brazenly exposed to view. Especially to his view.

Since he had come to Egypt he had grown accustomed to nudity. He had from the beginning disciplined himself to turn his eyes from it. Even when it was so flagrantly displayed, as Nefermati seemed determined to do, he had forced himself to ignore it. It was a struggle, but he was pleased that he had been able to master himself. *With the help of God,* he reminded himself.

Yet his very success in resisting her temptations had only spurred his master's wife to greater seductions. All the other household women had accepted Joseph's discipline. Only Nefermati continued to send out unspoken invitations.

"My lady, how may I serve you?" Joseph's words, as always with her, were formal.

"Come into the house with me, Joseph."

Her smile was friendly. Too friendly. They walked to the house, into the large commons room. Joseph followed her obediently, looking desperately for another servant. There was no one, it seemed, in the whole house.

"How is the inventory coming?" she asked.

"It is finished, my lady."

"Finished already? My, but you are clever!" She pressed

closer to him. He shied away. "What's the matter, Joseph? Don't you like me? Why can't you relax and be comfortable with me?"

"My lady, I am afraid."

"Afraid? Nonsense. I won't hurt you. I just want to be your friend."

Joseph did not like the way the conversation was going. "Thank you, my lady. But I am your slave."

"You're more than that, Joseph. You are the Chief Steward of the household. A position of honor. Doesn't that entitle you to be my . . . friend?"

The way she said "friend" frightened Joseph. The Egyptian word had a wide range of meanings. It could mean a casual acquaintance, anyone who wasn't your enemy. Or it could mean the intimate loved one who shared your bed. Which meaning she intended was not in doubt.

"My lady, please! Don't do this!"

The large soft eyes turned on him. "Do what, Joseph?" The words were innocent; the eyes were not.

"My lady, let us go outside. There are no others in the house now. I have many things I must do. *Please!*"

The last word was torn from his lips as a plea, as her fingers ran tantalizingly up and down his arms. Her lips pouted.

"Joseph, there's no one to see. Don't be so unfriendly. I am yours. Take me! Forget Potiphar. There's just you and me."

Her hands dropped to his schenti and tugged. The small knot which held it around the waist slipped free. It came loose in her hand.

Joseph panicked. He backed away, then turned and ran out of the house. Behind him he could hear the woman shrieking and calling his name. He was aware of his nakedness as he ran past some startled servants on his way to his own villa.

In his house, he got out another linen schenti and quickly put it on. Then he sat down on the floor and shuddered.

Nefermati. Beautiful child. Beautiful, yes, but child? No. Her bite was more poisonous than an asp.

He recalled the old Egyptian proverb: The only thing more dangerous than a mother lioness defending her cubs is a lioness the lion has rejected. Nefermati's rage at his rejection would mean the end of him. Just an hour ago, he had been excited about the success and prosperity of his stewardship in Potiphar's household, as revealed in the latest inventory.

His mind went to Nefermati. What she had done was understandable, in a way. Her husband was twenty years older than she, and away at Pharaoh's court much of the time. She was lonely. Her needs for sexual gratification were unfulfilled. The combination of boredom and sexual frustration had led her to this.

It was not uncommon. Most high-born ladies of Egypt carried on extramarital affairs, which were tolerated by their husbands. And it was no secret that Nefermati had many admirers she openly encouraged.

Even an affair with a slave was not unheard of. Joseph had recently heard about a wealthy nobleman who bought a Nubian slave and gave him to his wife for her amusement while he was away on a business trip. When he returned and found his wife pregnant, he had sent to the House of Life for a physician, who had given her a drug which had aborted the fetus. But he had kept the slave.

What would Potiphar have felt if Joseph had succumbed to her invitation? Resentment? Betrayal? Or calm amusement and tolerance?

After seven years of absorbing Egyptian culture, Joseph could still not accept the cultural morality which was so different from his training. His parents were strict about adultery and fornication. When Reuben had seduced his father's concubine, it caused a scandal for which Jacob had never fully forgiven his oldest son. When one of the natives of Shechem had seduced his half sister Dinah, his brothers had sworn vengeance. They not only killed the man, but his whole household as well.

In Joseph's family, morality was strict and harsh. These lessons had been burned deeply into his own code of ethics. Even after seven years of loose Egyptian morality, he could not see having an affair with his master's wife as anything other than a grievous sin.

God, where are you?

Just an hour ago, God was so close! For seven years God had richly blessed him and given him incredible good fortune. Was it all for nothing?

Where are you, God? Are you really with me? Or was it all an illusion, a balancing of the books in which the seven good years are now succeeded by seven bad ones?

"Joseph."

The familiar voice jerked his mind from his despairing thoughts. He looked up to see Potiphar standing in the doorway. He didn't know the master had come home.

He leaped to his feet, then impulsively went down on his knees and held out his arms at knee level. This was a gesture of obeisance from slave to master, but Potiphar had never required his slaves to do this. Particularly Joseph—their relationship was much too like father and son to require slave-master protocol.

"Stand up, Joseph."

Joseph rose to his feet. The words were kindly. His face was friendly, although grave. Joseph was taller than his master. But at that moment he felt shorter. For the first time in many years, he felt like a slave.

"Joseph, did you do it?"

A simple question. Joseph knew what it meant. Nefermati surely told her husband a story about being forced by his favorite slave, and the household servants would certainly support her story. Then there was Joseph's schenti in her hand, and perhaps a torn tunic of her own. It would certainly look like rape.

"No, Master. I did not."

Potiphar looked steadily at Joseph. "I believe you," he said. "I have known you seven years. I'm not likely to be fooled. And I know my wife." He shook his head sadly.

Joseph let out his breath slowly. His heart went out to the old man before him whom he loved so much.

"Sir," he said softly. "You'll have to do something. Perhaps send me away. We can't live under the same roof now. It will only happen again."

"I know, Joseph. But it's more serious than you think. The problem can't be solved merely by sending you away. She has asked for your death."

A cold finger of fear stabbed Joseph. Of course it was her right. It didn't make any difference if he were guilty or innocent. He was a slave, even if Chief Steward. But she was the mistress, the lady of the household. The lioness whom he had rejected.

"You must do your duty, sir."

"I know, Joseph," Potiphar sighed. "You will go immediately to the Royal Prison, where you will find User-Re. Explain the situation to him and have him place you under arrest. There's nothing else we can do."

"I understand, sir."

What he understood was that Potiphar trusted him completely. Ordinarily he would have summoned the house guards and sent the offending person off in chains. But this was a direct order to Joseph to take himself to prison. This trust reflected his master's deep affection for him.

"I'm sorry, Joseph." Potiphar's kindly face was grave. "It's hard for me. I have to choose between my wife and my . . . Chief Steward."

Joseph was sure he had meant to say "son." But that would never do.The master was placing his slave under arrest for an attempted rape of his wife. The word "son" would not fit the situation, no matter how deeply he felt.

Joseph quickly put on a linen kalasaris, which was a more formal attire than the schenti he wore around the house.

As he made his way out of the estate and through the streets of Avaris on his way to the prison, he was once again aware of that haunting question, posed so thoughtfully by his master seven years ago. "Is your God with you now?"

Are you, God? Is this the end of a beautiful dream? Was everything that happened these past seven years a lie? Where are you, God?

5

"Welcome to the Pharaoh's prison, Joseph. How may I serve the Chief Steward of the Lord Potiphar's house?"

User-Re, the captain of the guard in charge of the prison, sat on a low cushioned chair in his luxurious living quarters in the East Wing of the large prison building. He was a squat man, well-built, and although middle-aged still in athletic trim. His bald head and wrinkled face appeared deceptively old on top of his young-looking body.

"I am your prisoner," replied Joseph. "I have been placed under arrest by Potiphar himself. I am yours to command."

"By all the gods!" User-Re leaped to his feet, his eyes wide. "How can this be?"

Joseph briefly explained the circumstances of his arrest, including Nefermati's charge against him. His statement was a frank admission of guilt which did not accuse his former mistress.

User-Re grasped the situation immediately. Clashes between noble ladies and high-placed servants were not uncommon. Having met Nefermati and experiencing for himself her roving eyes and subtle sexual invitation, he knew perfectly well what had happened. What he did not understand was why Joseph had not accepted the invitation. He would have saved himself a lot of trouble.

But User-Re was more surprised by another aspect of

this interesting case. "Do you mean to tell me—" He paused and looked Joseph up and down, "—that the Lord Potiphar did not even call out his guards to bind you and drag you to prison? He just told you to report yourself under arrest to me? On your own?"

"Of course."

User-Re was silent for a moment, digesting this. He had observed the unusual relationship between the Pharaoh's Chief Executioner and his young Canaanite slave. The household crime of which he had been accused could result in his death. The captain of the guard blinked as he studied the handsome youth standing before him.

What he saw was an Egyptian noble, not a Canaanite slave. Joseph at age twenty-four looked and acted the part. His smooth-shaven head and face and even the white linen kalasaris which he wore were Egyptian. But User-Re saw more than that.

He saw a man of integrity and ability.

Integrity. What Joseph had just done—placing himself voluntarily under arrest and admitting the charge—User-Re had never seen before. He searched his mind for an ulterior motive which could produce for Joseph some personal gain. He could think of nothing.

And ability. Everyone in Avaris knew about Joseph, the slave who had risen so spectacularly in Potiphar's household. Some called it luck. Others speculated that Joseph's mysterious God had come down to Egypt and was helping him. Still others whispered that Potiphar was homosexual and Joseph was his lover. But most, including User-Re, simply believed Joseph's phenomenal rise was due to his unusual talent. His intelligence, industry, attention to details, and ability to command a staff of people marked him as a person favored by the gods.

And he was User-Re's prisoner. He rubbed his hands as the implication of this fact struck him. The sun god whom he worshiped and for whom he was named had sent him the answer to his prayers.

He smiled. "Welcome to the Pharaoh's prison, Joseph. You will be treated well here. You shall have a fine room in the East Wing. Put your mind at ease."

The soothing words were meant to calm Joseph. They produced the opposite effect. The prisoner frowned.

Joseph's quick mind grasped User-Re's intent. He had been to the prison before with his master. He was well aware of the three-tiered hierarchy existing here. The East Wing was not where he should be.

He should be in the West Wing, reserved for slaves. It consisted of one large room with a stone floor, and the prisoners were chained to the floor all over the room. No windows. Never cleaned and aired. As a result the place did not sustain life for long.

The afternoon sun baked the outside walls, and by sundown the temperature was over 110 degrees. The sweat and human excrement from crowded bodies made breathing almost impossible. Food and water were brought in once a day. Once a week a group of slaves came through and removed the dead bodies. Three weeks was the average life of a prisoner in the West Wing.

The North Wing was a little better, reserved for middle-class Egyptians and people who could afford to pay tribute to the jail administration. Occasionally a favorite slave of a noble was housed here, if his master paid enough. It was not freedom, but at least it was comfortable and the food good. Joseph had hoped to be housed in the North Wing, with arrangements made for Potiphar to pay the tribute.

The East Wing was a palace compared to the other two sections. User-Re and the other keepers of the prison had their own living quarters here. Occasionally a high-born noble or official of the court was "entertained" as a prisoner. This was where User-Re had assigned him. Why?

It didn't take Joseph long to guess. The shrewd captain of the guard needed a capable administrative assistant, someone who could straighten out the knotty problems of a complex prison system. The Chief Steward of the large house of Potiphar would have the experience and ability to fill the position.

With proper training, Joseph could completely take over the job now administered by the captain of the guard himself. This would free User-Re to indulge in his favorite sport: hunting birds in the papyrus thickets. No wonder Joseph seemed heaven-sent to User-Re.

User-Re called in his servant. "This is Joseph, who will stay with us for a while. Put him in one of the guest rooms and assign to him one of my slaves. Treat him well; he is an honored guest."

Joseph knew what "honored guest" meant—prisoner. Although he would have many privileges and even enjoy plush surroundings, he was still a prisoner. He remembered the night he had spent in the pit near Dothan hill many years ago. The terror of the night was still vivid in memory. Once again he was a prisoner, but his "pit" was a luxurious suite of rooms in the East Wing.

His personal servant reported to him, a young black slave from the land of Kush whose name was Kali. Although not particularly intelligent, the boy was quiet and obedient. During the first few days he expected to be beaten regularly. When he discovered that he had a very lenient master he became cheerful and attentive, fawning on Joseph like a puppy.

Joseph's work with User-Re began the next day. At first it consisted of routine scribe work, as Joseph learned the complex prison system administered by this servant of the Pharaoh. Joseph worked hard. In a few short months he had completely grasped the administration of the prison. Before a year had passed, User-Re was spending more time on hunting expeditions than he was at the prison.

As Joseph assumed more power, he began several far-reaching prison reforms. User-Re had no objections; in fact, he indulged this soft-hearted assistant administrator in everything he proposed. The prison was administered efficiently and with no serious problems. Why should he care what Joseph did? He was completely absorbed in learning to throw the boomerang which brought down choice birds in the papyrus swamps. He also had a growing number of well-trained hunting cats to make the sport less strenuous.

Joseph's first major project was to clean up the West Wing. He put the new prisoners to work doing this. Anyone who had been in that room for more than three or four days was in no condition to work. It took several weeks to shovel out the packed-down excrement and garbage on the floor.

Stone masons were brought in to cut windows in the walls high enough off the floor to prevent escape. Air holes were driven through the walls at floor level. Once a week the prisoners were made to scrub the floor, the excess water whisked out through the air holes. Fresh meat, fruit, and vegetables were brought in twice a day. The chained prisoners were led outside each day for exercise and a bath in the Great River. The mortality rate dropped considerably, and the large room began to overflow with prisoners.

Joseph then devised a system of farming out his prisoners for hard labor. The city of Avaris had been built only in the past century, and much construction work remained to be done. Pharaoh's builders accepted this arrangement readily, finding the prisoners a cheap source of labor. Joseph wondered often if any official in Pharaoh's court would object to this use of prisoners, but since they were mostly slaves, nobody seemed to care.

Rats had always been a problem in the prison. Joseph brought in an army of cats. The prisoners soon adopted them, feeding and petting and naming each one, especially after they saw the effect on the dwindling rat population.

In the North Wing where middle-class prisoners were kept, Joseph did not discontinue the purchase of favors from the prison guards. He took his cut as usual, but with the money he began a system which led to just trials for his prisoners. He retained several lawyers to keep their cases before the Pharaoh's court, with the result that these cases were not neglected and forgotten as they had been in the past. The turnover of prisoners was gratifying.

Potiphar frequently visited the prison. Joseph's reforms delighted him. Nefermati had forgotten about Joseph, and Potiphar would never remind her. Joseph was safe as long as she did not press charges.

And so the years slipped happily by for Joseph. He was comfortable and busy, and the work he did was important. He remembered wistfully the days of carefree life as a child, when he could dream his dreams of God's favoritism and his future destiny.

Was God with him now? Everything he did had been blessed by God. But where was it all leading? What was his future? Was he to be a prisoner forever?

Or did God have something in mind for him yet?

6

"My master's presence is requested in User-Re's living quarters."

Kali's words interrupted Joseph as he made preparations for Pharaoh's birthday, which was only sixteen days away. Each year on that festive day, Thebes celebrated at the Pharaoh's expense. For Joseph and the prison administration, it meant hard work. Pharaoh generally pardoned all prisoners in the East and North Wings. It was a time for cleaning house, before the prison began to fill up again.

He laid aside the papyrus scroll he was writing and turned to Kali—who was no longer a boy, he saw. Six years had passed since the black child from Kush had been assigned to him as his personal slave. He was a young man now. Perhaps Joseph should consider finding him a suitable wife. The next time an expedition returned from the land of Kush, he would purchase a new girl slave for him.

"I shall come right away, Kali."

Kali offered a fawning smile. The slave wasn't bright, but he was obedient and lovable.

In User-Re's living quarters, Joseph found the captain of the guard at home. There were also visitors. Two men, both elaborately dressed, wore the gold chain which meant they were employed in the service of the Pharaoh.

"Greetings, Joseph." User-Re's salutation was brief. He liked and respected Joseph but had made no attempt through the years to establish a friendly relationship. "We have two prisoners from the royal household."

Joseph bowed to the men. One was middle-aged, red-faced, and chubby. He cuddled a cat. The other was young, strikingly handsome, and with that honest open countenance which immediately inspired confidence.

"Welcome to the royal prison, honored guests. We shall try to make you as comfortable as possible.

The middle-aged chubby one spoke first. "Ah, Bastet! Bastet! You are kind! Thank you! And thank you too, Joseph. Thank you so much! You are most kind! Thank you, and thank you too, Bastet!"

Joseph smiled. Bastet was the cat goddess, worshiped by a few people scattered across Egypt and centered in a town on the Great River north of Avaris called Bubastis. Cat-goddess worshipers would naturally be fond of cats. This man had evidently picked up one of the many cats roaming the prison and befriended it.

The younger prisoner bowed respectfully before Joseph. "You are kind, sir." His quiet voice contrasted with the agitated nervousness of his fellow prisoner. "I am Thombos, chief baker in Pharaoh's household."

The chief baker filled a prestigious post. He had complete charge of the kitchens, which produced large volumes of quality food each day for the Pharaoh and the entire court. There were three times as many people to feed at the palace as at Potiphar's house. Joseph immediately appreciated the magnitude of this man's responsibility. About Joseph's age, he must be intelligent and capable to have risen this far in his young lifetime.

Before Joseph could reply, the cat-loving prisoner spoke again. "I should have introduced myself, Joseph. I'm sorry. I forgot. Oh, I'm so upset! I don't know what is going to happen to me! O, Bastet! Bastet! You must help me! Oh, excuse me. I'm forgetting again. My name is Bastakheren, and I am the Pharaoh's cupbearer. I have been accused of poisoning the Pharaoh's wine. O Bastet! Bastet! You know I am innocent!"

There was something pathetic yet likable about this man. He was truly frightened, and he stroked the cat's fur nervously, drawing strength and comfort from its presence.

"Be at ease, Bastakheren. Pharaoh's justice does not depend on whims and fancies. If you are innocent, the truth will come to light. All will be well. In the meantime, we will make you comfortable here at the royal prison."

Bastakheren opened his mouth to go into another voluble display of thanksgiving, but User-Re interrupted them. "Joseph, assign these men their quarters here in the East Wing. Give them each a slave for a personal servant. You must make them as comfortable as their royal station permits."

Joseph bowed to User-Re, then turned to the two prisoners. "Come this way, sirs. I will show you your quarters."

He turned to go but was startled when Bastakheren said in a soothing voice, "Come along, User-Re, that's a good boy."

What an odd thing to say. Joseph looked back. Bastakheren was talking to the cat! Evidently it was the name he had given his adopted cat. User-Re—the man—chuckled and Joseph relaxed. He turned and led the way out.

"You are fortunate," he said to Bastakheren a few minutes later after they had explored his new living quarters. "User-Re has a sense of humor. He might have been offended at your naming a cat after him."

"Oh I'm sure he doesn't mind." Bastakheren stroked the cat before letting him down on the floor of his new quarters. "I talked with him about it before you came. It is an honor to have a cat named for you. It means Bastet knows your name and will watch over you. I told your captain this. He seemed pleased. Or amused, I don't know which. Anyway, I plan to name a cat for you, Joseph."

"Thank you. And now I must show Thombos his quarters." For all his flightiness and volubility, Bastakheren was a likable person. Joseph wished him well.

After he had shown Thombos around his plush apartment, Joseph was surprised when the chief baker asked him to stay a minute. They seated themselves before the window overlooking a courtyard. Thombos' new servant served them wine.

"I have a favor to ask of you." Thombos' earnest face was grave.

"I shall be glad to help, if I can."

"Would you send word to my wife about my predicament? Please tell her in such a way that she will not worry too much. If you do, I shall be most grateful."

"I'll do so immediately. Where does she live?"

"She and our two children live in a small but comfortable house on the Street of the Palms, near the new canal. Would you please let her know I'm innocent of any wrongdoing? When this is discovered, I will be released."

"Of course." Joseph looked into his anguished young face and wished he didn't feel a strange foreboding about this personable man. "Is there anything else I can do?"

Thombos' smile fluttered over his mouth. "No, I'm sure everything will resolve itself in a few days. My chief assistant was careless and served the Pharaoh some tainted meat, causing temporary sickness. The Pharaoh accused me of poisoning him and ordered me to prison."

"But didn't you explain that it was your assistant's fault?"

"Perhaps I should have. But I didn't want to get the man into trouble. He's not an evil man—just careless. It happened while I was absent from the kitchens and at home with my wife, who was giving birth to our second child. Maybe I should have stayed at the palace that day. But when the Pharaoh learns the truth, I shall be freed."

Joseph stroked his chin as he looked at the chief baker. The assistant, evidently an inefficient cook, had not inspected carefully the piece of meat he would prepare for the Pharaoh. Then Thombos had covered up for him, taking the blame so his assistant wouldn't bear the brunt of Pharaoh's wrath. Perhaps not a wise thing to do. Possibly even a dangerous thing. But Joseph was forced to admire the man who was his prisoner.

"I shall send someone to your wife immediately." He stood to go. "Meanwhile, make yourself comfortable. I'm sure your problem will be resolved in due time."

"Thank you." Thombos placed his hand on Joseph's shoulder, an unusual thing for a high-born noble to do to an inferior, a slave. It was a sign of friendship. "You have made me feel much better. I hope I may serve you some day."

Joseph left with a continued feeling of uneasiness. He made a mental note to talk to Potiphar about this man, to discover what could be done for him at Pharaoh's court, if anything. People had been executed for less cause than this.

He sent a silent prayer to God for help. The feeling of foreboding had eased, but he wasn't completely comfortable. He wished he could do more.

7

There were three days left before Pharaoh's birthday.

Joseph had worked hard during the past two weeks in preparation. All was ready now. Lists of prisoners had been submitted, under the seal of User-Re, for the royal commission's approval. Joseph was sure all his recommendations would be accepted. Now he would have to wait.

And relax.

His mind turned to the two prisoners from the royal household, both of whom were on his list for pardon. He had had very little contact with them during the past two weeks. Too bad. Both were cheerful and likable, and Joseph had hoped to get better acquainted with them. The press of duties had prevented him.

Now he had a free moment. He called his servant.

"Kali, go to the living quarters of Bastakheron and Thombos. Invite them to come for a visit. Then bring us some wine and honey cakes, and arrange for a few fans to move the air."

Joseph had learned much about his two prisoners. As he waited for his guests to come, he thought about each one's case.

Bastakheren.

The royal cupbearer was a popular figure in the court. "Buba," they called him at the royal palace. The nickname was a shortened form of Bubastis, the cat-city on the Nile where Bastakheren had come from. The name "Buba" was an affectionate term of respect and intimacy. Everyone spoke of him fondly.

Joseph had also learned that Buba was a shrewd and capable man. The position of cupbearer was more than just an honorary one. At all banquets he stood by Pharaoh's table and tasted every cup of wine and every dish of food which came before the Pharaoh. But his job entailed much more. He had risen to be in charge of many activities in the palace, from managing the household servants to supervising the maintenance and cleaning chores of the building itself. Buba was meticulous and conscientious; the palace was immaculate.

The chief baker, Thombos, was less well known. He worked behind the scenes in Pharaoh's kitchens, a monumental job. Well over a hundred slaves and skilled workers made up the kitchen staff. From experience Joseph could appreciate the enormous task of gathering food from Pharaoh's country estates, preparing it in the various divisions of the vast kitchen, and bringing it all together in a colorful and appetizing meal twice a day. Thombos, he had heard, worked hard at his job. Never before had Pharaoh found cause for complaint.

Potiphar had told him recently of rumors of trouble in the kitchen. The palace was always full of intrigue, which even extended into the kitchen staff. The chief assistant, a vain and ambitious man, coveted the position of chief baker. Now he was telling everyone who would listen that Thombos was the Pharaoh's poisoner.

The ingratitude of the man disgusted Joseph. Thombos had covered for his assistant's carelessness. Now the assistant was taking advantage of Thombos' absence to plot against him. Thombos had many friends in the royal household, and there were counter-rumors and counterplots. But Thombos himself was not there, and the assistant was.

Joseph had also learned of Thombos' family. Kali had reported that his visit to the little house on the Street of Palms was a pleasant one. Thombos' wife had been cordial to him and grateful to Joseph for sending the message. The two little boys, ages two and four, were stalwart healthy youngsters with good manners. Kali painted for Joseph a loving domestic picture. He hoped Thombos would be able to enjoy it for many years to come.

"Greetings, Joseph, my good friend. May Bastet honor you today!"

Buba had arrived first. He immediately launched into a long and wordy account of the new cat he had acquired and promptly named "Joseph." The cat goddess was smiling on Joseph now. Couldn't he feel it?

When Thombos arrived, he too smiled as he bowed respectfully to both Joseph and Buba. "Greetings, Joseph. It was thoughtful of you to invite us here, just three days before Pharaoh's birthday. I know how busy you have been."

Joseph led them to the window overlooking the garden. There they sat on low cushioned benches. Behind them slaves waved ostrich fans. Kali brought a jar of wine and small cups for each one, then placed before them a large plate of date-honey cakes.

"My friends," said Joseph, smiling at his guests, "are you comfortable in your quarters? I hope there are at least as many servants to wait upon your needs as there are cats in Buba's room."

Buba laughed. "Ah, Joseph. In Bubastis we have a saying, 'When your cats outnumber your servants, you are wealthy.' If that is so, my wealth exceeds that of both of you!"

Thombos smiled. "I too am comfortable, even if my servants outnumber my cats. Although I have to admit, I have not slept well these past few nights."

Joseph's smile disappeared. "Is something wrong, my friend!"

"No, no. Nothing serious. But I have been troubled by my dreams lately. They're the kind of dreams that must mean something, but I have no idea what."

Joseph picked up a cake. "Maybe I can help. I know something about that kind of dream. I had them during my childhood. The God I worship made them clear. Maybe if you tell your dreams, I can interpret them for you."

"I've had dreams, too." Buba would not be left out. "Just last night I dreamt there were three vines before me, loaded with grapes. I took the grapes in my hands, squeezed them into the royal cup, and handed them to the Pharaoh. He drank deeply."

Joseph smiled. "What a pleasant dream." He looked at his two guests, deciding to make a cheerful parlor game of this dream business. "The three vines are three days. In three days you will be free. Soon you will be handing the Pharaoh his wine cup again."

"Joseph, do you think so? Really? Thank you, Bastet! Thank you, thank you! And thank you too, Joseph! May Bastet reward you. Thank you!"

Joseph laughed, but Thombos gazed at Joseph solemnly. "How do you do that, Joseph? Your God must surely speak to you, if you can interpret dreams as easily as that."

Joseph shook his head, smiling. "There's no secret, my friends. Three vines—three days. Why not? Everybody knows Pharaoh's birthday is coming then, and I expect him to extend his pardon to Buba and restore him to his former position. I wish all dreams were as plain as this!"

Buba bubbled with excitement. "Bastet be praised! Three more days and I shall be free. Joseph, you are remarkably blessed by your God. Now, tell us about your dream, Thombos."

Thombos took a sip of wine, smiling broadly. "My dream I hope is equally easy to interpret. I dreamt that I carried three wicker baskets on my head, each filled with loaves of bread. Then birds flew down and began to peck at the bread through the wicker sides of the basket. Soon the bread was gone, leaving me with empty baskets. Now, Joseph, what does it mean?"

Joseph felt a chill. What had started out as a game, a little harmless party conversation, had suddenly become threatening. This dream had too many negative overtones.

"Thombos, we've been playing a game with dream interpretation, nothing more. I have no magical powers, like Pharaoh's magicians claim for themselves. I believe in my God, but God's ways are mysterious. No one can be sure what a dream means."

"Joseph, speak plainly. Tell me the meaning of my dream."

Joseph hesitated. He could not lie to his friend. But he sensed in his soul the truth of the dream. Its meaning forced itself on him so clearly, so unmistakably, that he could not deny it. Telling Thombos would be like hitting him over the head with a war club.

He avoided his friend's eyes. Then he turned and gazed out the window. Behind him, no one spoke, waiting for him to tell them the meaning of his dream.

When he spoke, his voice was soft. "The three baskets, of course are the three days. But then. . . ." His voice faltered, and he could say no more. He didn't need to. In that moment of silence, the swishing of the ostrich fans could be heard.

"I see." Thombos' voice shook. "Do you think it may be true, Joseph?"

"I certainly hope not. But I have a very bad feeling about it."

Thombos rose and walked over to the window. He

stared out for a moment, then turned back to Joseph. "What shall I do?"

"I don't know." Joseph himself had been stunned by his revelation, which he could not deny had come from God. He made a sudden decision. "There is one thing I *can* do. It isn't much, I'm afraid. But I don't know what else—"

Thombos turned and looked at Joseph hopefully. Joseph continued. "I shall send to the Street of the Palms and bring your wife and two children here. This may be contrary to prison rules, but no one shall know. They will stay in your quarters for the next three days. You shall not be disturbed."

"Thank you, Joseph. You are kind."

Joseph shook his head and tried to smile. "It may be for nothing, Thombos. Maybe I'm completely mistaken about this. If you *are* released on Pharaoh's birthday, at least no harm will have been done by your family's visit. Then we can all have a good laugh about this. I sincerely hope that will be the case."

"So do I."

"And I." Buba spoke for the first time. His normally cheerful face was creased in a frown. "And I shall say a prayer to Bastet for you, my friend."

Joseph's guests soon left to return to their quarters. What had begun as a pleasant party had ended in gloom.

Joseph knew he must go himself to the house in the Street of the Palms to bring Thombos' wife to the prison. This was much too important to entrust to Kali. He would go at once. He called Kali to him and instructed him to arrange for a squad of soldiers to accompany them. Then with Kali as his guide, he went to the Street of the Palms.

The house was a pleasant little structure shaded by palm trees. Thombos' wife was a pretty girl, rather vivacious, but awed by the visit of Joseph and his retinue. She invited Joseph inside.

Quickly Joseph explained the purpose of his visit. He told of their party game, and how the dream interpretation seemed to be valid, although he hoped not. Thombos' wife paled, but she took it calmly, which impressed Joseph. He had expected her to moan and wail. Instead, she excused herself to gather her two children and a few things they would need for a three-day visit.

While she was gone, Joseph glanced around the room. In the corner, a statue of the god Bes dominated the room. He had seen them before and knew that the god's appearance was deceiving. Although squat, ugly and deformed, it represented domestic happiness. Joseph had observed that Bes worshipers were responsible people. They held high the virtues of love and tenderness for their spouse.

Joseph frowned, recalling that Bes was also known as the bringer of joy and protector against evil.

Would this god be able to protect this household?

Joseph shuddered. Unlike the Egyptians, he did not believe in pantheism. He had been raised to believe in one true God. All other gods were false except the one his family worshiped. The god Bes had nothing to do with molding a man's character; rather, the kind of people who would choose to follow Bes were people of high character anyway. But Bes could not help anyone, since he did not even exist.

Your ways are mysterious, O God. If your dream-revelation is indeed true, I shall not question you. You are God. Just lead me to be of some help to this good man.

During the next three days, Joseph became ever more convinced that his interpretation of the dreams had been correct. He heard more rumors from the palace of the kitchen intrigue, including the testimony of the assistant baker about catching Thombos in the act of trying to poison the Pharaoh's food. Thombos was not even asked for his side of it. On Pharaoh's birthday, Joseph was not surprised when Potiphar appeared before him.

"Pharaoh's justice has been pronounced, Joseph. Deliver to me the prisoner Thombos."

"Justice!" Joseph could not keep the bitterness from his voice. "The man is innocent. The assistant baker is an ungrateful liar. There's no justice in this act."

The chief executioner nodded his head slowly. "Nevertheless, it is Pharaoh's will, and his will is law. I must do my duty. But if it will make you feel better, that other prisoner—the cupbearer—has been cleared of all charges and will return to active duty in the palace."

So it was true then. The dreams *were* signs from God. He felt awed that he had this remarkable power. But the awe left him as he remembered Thombos, now waiting with his wife and two children to hear his fate.

"Potiphar, if you must do this, please make it swift and painless."

"I shall, Joseph." It was almost a rebuke, for Potiphar had always carried out his duties in the most humane way possible.

There was no putting it off. Joseph and Potiphar slowly marched toward the East Wing on their sorrowful mission.

8

The Pharaoh Sutekh leaned back on his cedar throne and surveyed his court.

He prided himself on his reputation as a "Shepherd-king." His grandfather had led the invasion into Egypt which had swept the foreigners before them. The weak rulers of Egypt were no match for the swift chariots, the skilled bowmen, and the bronze swords. All resistance had crumbled before the fierce energy of the invaders.

His grandfather had established his temporary capitol at Memphis, intending to push further south and make the ancient city of Thebes the permanent home for the new dynasty of the Shepherd-kings. The entrenched Pharaoh there had opposed him. He had been forced to consolidate and establish himself in the upper half of Egypt. That was when he built his new city, Avaris, hoping it would outshine Thebes in grandeur and beauty.

Pharaoh Sutekh smiled grimly to himself. Like his grandfather and father before him, he had adopted much of the culture of Egypt, retaining the austere military discipline of the dynasty of the mighty Shepherd-kings. It was a good marriage: the sophisticated culture of Egypt and the military might of his people.

The throne on which he sat had once been a cedar tree in the land of his origins, but the dais and floor on which it stood were Egyptian marble. The nobles, the scribes, the courtesans who surrounded him had the look of Egypt. But underneath, he knew, they were of the stern character of his ancestors.

His was the only chair on the dais. His courtiers stood around him on the lower level. On his left just off the platform was Bastakheron, the royal cupbearer, whom everyone called Buba. Two years had passed since his release from prison.

The Pharaoh was troubled. Ordinarily the first thing he did when he sat on his throne each morning was pray to Seth. This was his stern pig-faced god whom the Egyptians claimed murdered their weak god Osiris.

He often followed his prayer with a brief homily on the greatness of his god. Seth, so much like one of the gods his ancestors had worshiped, was the only god in the Egyptian pantheon who understood the true rulers of Egypt, the Shepherd-kings.

But this morning, he did not even say his morning prayer.

"Call in the wizards!"

Buba bustled out to obey. He dispatched slaves who scurried off in every direction to bring in the collection of magicians, fortune-tellers, dream interpreters, and necromancers left over from the former Pharaoh's reign. The present Pharaoh usually ignored them, but he kept them around in case he was confronted by an insurmountable problem, as now. He took dreams seriously—and knew instinctively that his vision last night was an important revelation involving the administration of his kingdom.

Soon Buba ushered in an array of strangely clad men, who paraded past the silver pool with the three fountains. They took their places before the Pharaoh's dais throne, then went to their knees and stretched out their hands at knee level before the Pharaoh.

"O king, live forever!" The usual formal greeting in the

royal chamber rumbled in unison from all of them. Then a dark-robed bearded man in a conical cap, obviously from a faraway mysterious land, spoke for all of them. "May the fierce god Seth smile on you this day and every day! How may we serve you, great sovereign?"

The Pharaoh's subdued voice could scarcely be heard above the splashing of the three fountains. "I had two dreams last night. You will tell me what they mean."

The wizards looked at each other in dismay. They were not very good at extemporaneous magic-making. Their tricks and schemes took hours to prepare. "We will do our best, my Lord Pharaoh," said the bearded one.

Pharaoh Sutekh's voice was so low that everyone in the hall had to strain to hear him.

"I dreamed last night about seven cows. They were fat and healthy as they came up out of the Great River and began to graze in a nearby pasture. Then came seven more cows, lean and hungry, with their ribs showing. The seven lean cows attacked the seven fat cows and ate them up. That's when the dream ended and I woke."

Again there was dismay on the faces of the wizards, but Pharaoh was not finished.

"I dreamed again. This time I saw a grainfield, and especially one stalk of grain. It had seven heads of grain on it, all good healthy clusters. Then as I watched, seven other heads began to grow on the same stalk. They were ugly and diseased, and they took over and devoured the seven healthy grain buds."

The Pharaoh leaned forward on his throne. He seemed young, even in his wig and artificial beard, which the Shepherd-kings had adopted in his grandfather's time. He looked directly at the wizards and spoke sharply one word. "Interpret!"

The chief wizard stammered, "O great Pharaoh, your dream is . . . well . . . we will need time to study your dreams. Yes, time. We need to consult the oracles, commune with the dark powers, examine entrails, perhaps fast—"

"Enough!" Pharaoh's growled. "Either you know what it means, or you don't! Tell me . . . *now!"*

"My Lord Pharaoh, have mercy! We need time to study it."

"Get out of my sight, you charlatans! You know nothing."

The wizards backed out past the silver pool and soon were lost among the wooden columns at the far end of the audience hall. The Pharaoh sat brooding on the throne. No one dared speak.

Except Buba.

The chubby cupbearer stepped forward before the dais and awkwardly went down on his knees with his hands stretched out at knee level. "O king, live forever!" he intoned. "May I offer a suggestion?"

The Pharaoh laughed shortly. "What do you know about dreams, cupbearer?"

"Nothing, my lord Pharaoh. But I know someone who does."

"Ah!" Pharaoh Sutekh sat up straight on his throne. "Tell me!"

Buba lifted is head but remained on his knees. "Two years ago, when I was sent to prison for a short time, I met a man there named Joseph. He is the assistant administrator of the prison. I had a dream which he interpreted accurately for me, foretelling my release."

"That may have been an accident. How do you know his interpretation wasn't a lucky guess?"

"Do you remember the chief baker, Thombos, who was executed at the time I was released? Joseph interpreted his dream also, which accurately foretold his execution. My lord, this man is incredible. I swear by Bastet he is!"

Ordinarily Pharaoh did not permit anyone to mention another god's name other than his own Seth, but the Pharaoh liked Buba enough to allow him liberties. And Sutekh was not interested in god's names at this moment.

"Bring him to me!"

Buba scrambled to his feet and hurried out. In the silence that followed, the splashing of the fountains sounded loudly in the crowded hall.

Then Pharaoh spoke. "Does anybody here know this Joseph?"

Potiphar, the chief executioner, was present among the courtiers. He stood at the side, beside a wooden column alive with brightly colored pictures of birds and flowers. He spoke immediately.

"O king, live forever! I know him!"

He hurried forward and knelt on the floor, stretching out his hands at knee level. Pharaoh nodded, the signal for Potiphar to rise. Unlike the weak Pharaohs of the upper half of Egypt, Sutekh did not require his subjects to remain prostrate before him.

Potiphar paused. Then he took a deep breath and began. "Joseph came to me thirteen years ago as a slave, seventeen years of age, from a family of shepherds in the land of Canaan."

Potiphar paused, but he did not fail to notice the Pharaoh's interest in Joseph's shepherd background and place of origin. He continued.

"He had a good mind and was eager to learn, so I turned him over to my scribe to learn the language. Within two years he could not only speak Egyptian, but had mastered both the hieratic script and the hieroglyphic writings. He could easily write classical documents. He could do a large part of the arithmetic required for—"

He was interrupted by a snort from one of the courtiers, which drew the attention of the Pharaoh and everyone else. The man was the Pharaoh's scribe. He went down on his knees beside Potiphar and made his obeisance. "O king, live forever!" At Pharaoh's nod, he rose and spoke.

"What he describes is impossible, my lord Pharaoh. Scribes go to school for many years to learn this. No one can learn that much in just two years!"

"Nevertheless, it is true!" Potiphar spoke boldly. "This young man is remarkable. He learned much in that short time, so much that I assigned him to be my assistant steward. He not only did his job well but began to assume more and more responsibilities in my household until he had completely taken over the position of Chief Steward. And he was the best steward I ever had."

"If that is so," said the scribe, his eyes narrowing, "then why is he not still your steward? He is in prison, I believe."

"It is true, lord Pharaoh. There was a . . . misunderstanding between him and my wife. I had to incarcerate him. It was no fault of his."

Potiphar's hesitation was plain to everybody in the room. They could easily guess what had happened. Potiphar's wife Nefermati was well known at the palace, and her reputation for flirtation and extramarital affairs was legendary. It took no great imagination to conclude that Joseph rejected Nefermati's advances, and she had caused the trouble which led to Joseph's imprisonment.

The obvious question was asked by Pharaoh himself. "Then why has he not been put to death? You said he was a slave. Why is he still living?"

Potiphar was ready with an answer. He hurried on, thankful to leave painful subject of his wife's infidelities. "He is too outstanding a man to be wasted. User-Re, the captain of the guard at the royal prison, saw his value immediately and appointed him his assistant in the prison administration. The young man's intelligence and experience as a household steward were invaluable to User-Re."

Pharaoh nodded. "We all know of User-Re. He is one of the finest prison administrators ever to hold that position. His prison reforms have often drawn our commendation."

"User-Re is a shrewd man, my lord Pharaoh. He is able to recognize a talented man when he sees one and make good use of him. Such is the case with Joseph. It is Joseph, not User-Re, who makes the administration of the royal prison system run so smoothly. User-Re's great talent is in recognizing and using Joseph's talent!"

"And what god does this remarkable man worship?"

"He has his own God, who is known only in the land of Canaan, and is claimed by only one family. The name of this God is unknown—or else is too sacred to be spoken in the presence of nonbelievers. He has no image but is a spirit. This is a Creator-God, who even now controls everything that happens. Or so Joseph says, because he gives all the credit for his successes to his God."

"So." Sutekh leaned back on his throne to consider this. "This Joseph—he must be a unique person, even if he does not recognize who is the strongest god in Egypt. I am looking forward to meeting him."

He didn't have long to wait. Just then Buba burst through the colonnade at the end of the audience hall with another man. The second man's long confident stride contrasted sharply with Buba's erratic bustle. The clean open face beneath the hastily donned wig inspired confidence.

Joseph had been in Egypt long enough to know what he must do. He came before the dais throne and went down on his knees, stretching out his hands at knee level. Then at Pharaoh's nod, he rose and looked the royal personage directly in the eye.

"O king, live forever." Then he added a benediction of his own. "May God bless you and enrich your life this day and every day!"

A sudden stillness pervaded the hall. All the courtiers

knew what Sutekh believed. Seth was the only god who had the power of the Shepherd-kings behind him. The Pharaoh did not allow other gods to be mentioned in his presence. Buba had gotten away with it a few minutes before, but Buba was Buba. This was a stranger. What Joseph had said almost amounted to blasphemy. There was a low buzz of conversation.

But Pharaoh only stared at Joseph in stony silence. No one knew his thoughts as he regarded this upstart.

What the Pharaoh was actually thinking would have surprised everyone in the palace.

He saw before him a Canaanite, a man whose origins were similar to his own. He saw a man of intelligence and noble bearing, whose proud carriage showed no fear. He saw a man who worshiped a new God, a God so different from the usual pantheon of Egyptian and Canaanite gods as to merit some scrutiny. Perhaps this God would even offer new revelations. This must be a man through whom a God spoke.

Besides, the Pharaoh was desperate. His dreams had deeply troubled him. He must know their meaning. Perhaps the future well-being of his realm depended on this.

"Thank you, Joseph. You are welcome here. Perhaps your God will speak to us all today."

What an unusual thing to say! There were many raised eyebrows in the room. But even more went up at Pharaoh's next words.

"Joseph, I am sure you will be able to interpret my dreams."

"My lord Pharaoh, dreams are known only to God. Maybe God will allow me to interpret. God has in the past. I shall be gratified if I can be of service to you in this way."

Pharaoh shifted on his throne. "Yes. I look forward to hearing what God has to say through you."

Again, the raised eyebrows among the courtiers. This

was most unusual for their Pharaoh, to accept so readily a foreign god, as well as a person who spoke for him.

When Pharaoh raised his voice, it reflected the tension he felt.

"Hear, then, my dreams. Seven cows came out of the Great River and began to eat the grass in a nearby pasture. These cows were sleek and fat, looking healthy and well-fed. Then came seven more cows, thin and hungry-looking, with their ribs showing. The lean cows proceeded to eat the fat cows. That was my first dream.

"The second dream was of a stalk of grain in the field. It had seven healthy buds on it. As I watched, there began to grow on the same stalk seven more buds of grain, diseased, ugly, and stale. The unhealthy grain devoured the healthy grain on the stalk. Such were my dreams. Now what does your God say they mean?"

Joseph quickly sensed the meaning of the dream. He spoke without hesitation.

"My lord Pharaoh, the dreams both mean the same thing. There will be seven years of plenty, when the cattle will increase and the grainfields will overflow with rich harvests.

"The years of plenty will be followed by seven years of famine, as the land will not yield a good crop. The seven lean years will be disastrous, and will bring much suffering, causing everyone to forget the seven good years."

There was a gasp of disbelief among the courtiers. Joseph had spoken so confidently that many of them were convinced he was bluffing. It would not be difficult to invent an explanation and put it forth boldly. At that moment, there was no proof this interpretation was right or wrong, but they thought Joseph was taking a terrible chance. If his interpretation proved wrong—and it undoubtedly would, because it forecast impossible, unheard-of crop conditions—Joseph would be in big trouble.

Only three people in the whole room believed him—Potiphar, Buba, and the Pharaoh himself. But the Pharaoh was sovereign. His vote was the only one that counted.

"And what would you advise, Joseph?"

"My lord Pharaoh, you have been graciously warned by God of what will happen. And you must prepare for it. May I respectfully suggest that you appoint the wisest man in your kingdom to be the Grain Administrator. That man will carefully store up all the extra grain produced in the seven prosperous years immediately ahead of us.

"Then in the seven years of famine, he can distribute it as he sees fit. This will not only save your kingdom from starvation but will bring you more power and wealth than all your armies and conquests. You will have an economic sword in your hand which will conquer everything!"

Again there were gasps of disbelief, followed by a spontaneous burst of agitated conversation. This man was going too far! But Pharaoh stood, raising his scepter.

"Let there be silence in the court. I will make a proclamation!"

Instantly the room grew quiet; the water splashing in the pool could be heard. Pharaoh waited for a dramatic moment, then launched into his proclamation.

"Bring forth a gold chain and place it around his neck!"

Buba hastened to do his bidding. He knew about the supply of chains kept in a treasure box behind the throne. The gold chain was a sign of honor and could be worn only by the nobles of the realm. But Sutekh wasn't finished.

He frowned, pursing his lips in concentration. He stared out over the heads of the now-quiet assembly, as though gathering his thoughts. Finally he nodded and turned once again to Joseph.

He removed the large ring from his finger. "Place this ring on his finger."

The gasp in the hall this time was one of astonishment, as Buba hastened forward. Stepping on the dais, he took the ring from Pharaoh and placed it on Joseph's finger.

The courtiers were aghast. The signet ring! A gold chain was one thing, for most of them wore the Pharaoh's gold chain themselves. It bestowed an extremely high honor on a former slave and prison inmate. It elevated him immediately to a peer of the realm.

But the signet ring!

Only one other person in the kingdom was entitled to wear one of these rings. He was Enkhu, the Vizier, whose word in lower Egypt was law. When he made a decree, dictated it to a scribe, and affixed the seal of the signet ring on it, it became the law of the land. Only the Pharaoh himself could strike it down.

Now Joseph had a signet ring on his finger. It could mean only one thing: Joseph was suddenly one of the most powerful men in all Egypt, equal to Enkhu. His power was surpassed only by the Pharaoh himself.

Into the stunned silence, Pharaoh spoke. "Here is my decree. Joseph shall be appointed immediately to the position of Grain Administrator for a period of fourteen years. During that time, his power shall be my power. Let it be done. And let it be written, for it is God's will."

The shock of Joseph's sudden elevation was equaled by the shock of Pharaoh referring to Joseph's God.

But Pharaoh was still not finished. He raised his scepter again. All eyes turned toward him.

"You are no longer Joseph." His voice now rang with confidence. "You are henceforth to be called Zaphenath-paneah. So let it be!"

The courtiers' eyes turned from Pharaoh to Joseph, who by this time was on his knees, his head bowed, his arms stretched out at knee level.

The name meant "God speaks" and "He lives." There

was awe and wonder written on their faces as they gazed silently at this prostrate young man. The name explained a lot. Amazingly, Pharaoh Sutekh must believe that Joseph's God spoke through this man.

The Pharaoh further believed that there were now two voices of authority in Egypt: Seth, who spoke through Sutekh, and Joseph's God, who spoke through Joseph. Whether it was true or not, the Pharaoh evidently believed it. And suddenly the course of the rule of the Shepherd-kings and the history of Egypt had turned a corner.

Joseph lay prostrate on the floor before Pharaoh's raised scepter. He was stunned. His numbed mind could scarcely accept it. His confused thoughts raced back to the night in the pit at Dothan hill, when his assurance of the presence of God was shattered. Gradually he had recovered that awareness as the years had passed in Egypt. But he still wasn't sure. Even when he discovered the strange power to interpret dreams, he was still not quite sure.

Now he was.

He knew beyond any doubt that God was with him.

Joseph remained kneeling prostrate on the floor, arms stretched out at knee level. Only he, in all that company gathered in the great palace of the Shepherd-kings, knew that his obeisance was not before the Pharaoh, but before the great God he worshiped.

"I am yours to command, O God," he whispered. "I will do as you direct."

9

Six months had passed since the day which turned Joseph's life around.

"O king, live forever!" Joseph knelt with his arms stretched out at knee level. "May God give you the peace and prosperity which you seek for Egypt."

Pharaoh smiled. "He certainly gave me both peace and prosperity when he sent you to me, Zaphenath-paneah."

In spite of the informal surroundings, Pharaoh still used Joseph's formal name. During the last six months, he had never called Joseph anything else.

Pharaoh Sutekh sat on a low cushioned chair in his personal chambers. His private apartment was a palace in itself, separate from the other four residences in the vast royal palace. Here the Pharaoh gave small audiences and conducted private business.

Joseph arose. He had made considerable progress during his six months as Grain Administrator and was eager to report it.

"My lord Pharaoh," he began confidently. "The first great harvest is under way. On schedule."

"Start from the beginning, please." The Pharaoh sighed. "Tell me everything you have done."

Joseph was mildly surprised at this. He had been told by Buba that Pharaoh did not like to listen to long reports and conduct business which he considered tedious. Sutekh was an able administrator but preferred to carefully select capable men to carry on the practical chores of running a kingdom.

That was why Sutekh had selected Enkhu to be his Vizier. Joseph had never met a more astute man. His careful attention to detail in the day-to-day administration of the kingdom and foreign affairs enabled Pharaoh Sutekh to spend more time with his soldiers, watching them rehearse chariot maneuvers or practice swordplay.

Joseph had condensed his report so that his sovereign would not have to listen to a detailed account.

"Hear then this progress report. My first job was to recruit thirty-five men to be my assistants. They are mostly recent graduates of the scribe school. All are bright young men of promise. I assigned them their tasks."

Pharaoh nodded absently. Joseph hurried on.

"I sent them out over all the Black Lands, including the southern kingdom where the lesser Pharaoh rules because of your tolerance. They talked to every farmer and landowner, encouraging them to plant as much grain as they could this year. They were given extra amounts of seed. Each farmer was promised that the government would buy his entire crop at the current rate."

Joseph paused. Was he going into too much detail? He would have to omit statistics. He plunged ahead.

"When my assistants reported to me their response, I concluded that the present number of warehouses for storage of grain would hold only about half the crop. So I began immediately to build new grain silos. By the time they are completed, the crop will be ready for harvest."

Joseph did not need to tell the Pharaoh that Egypt had the ideal climate for storing grain. In a properly built silo, wheat, barley, and corn could be preserved almost indefinitely.

"I then realized this would take care of only the first

year, with six more to come. When the farmers find out we really do intend to purchase their crops, they will plant more and more in future years. Therefore I have begun the erection of many more storehouses scattered up and down the Great River." He paused. "A large project."

"And an expensive one." Pharaoh did not ordinarily concern himself with such trivialities as financing. The tribute from upper Egypt alone far exceeded his needs. The wealth of Egypt was so great, it was beyond Sutekh's practical mind to comprehend. Joseph wondered why he would even comment on the expense of building new grain silos. It was a tiny amount compared to the total income of his vast empire.

But Joseph knew why. Only one thing absorbed Pharaoh Sutekh's attention: world conquest. His empire even now stretched all the way north to the land of the Ammoru and eastward to the Twin Rivers. Other Shepherd-kings ruled in these places, but they thought of it as just one vast empire. Their total wealth was unknown. What was important now was not military but economic control.

Was this Pharaoh, Joseph wondered, astute enough to recognize that all the military power in the world was not equal to the economic control he would have if Joseph's interpretation of his dreams came true?

Joseph then knew what he must say to his sovereign.

"My lord Pharaoh, please think of it as an investment. When the seven years of famine begin, you will have complete control of the grain market. You will become enormously powerful.

"People will come from everywhere wanting grain, bringing their money. They will beg for peace, knowing this is the price they must pay for your generosity."

Pharaoh's eyes bored into Joseph's for a moment. Then he lifted them to the ceiling and sighed. "I entrust things like that to you. You're guided by your God, I know."

Strange, mused Joseph, how Pharaoh Sutekh, when confronted by concepts beyond his understanding, assigned their explanation to God. For that matter, so did Joseph. The difference between Joseph's and the Pharaoh's approaches was that Joseph also saw God as present in everything he *did* understand.

"There is another step we can take, my lord Pharaoh." Now was the time to speak to his sovereign about the plan which his active mind had been working on for weeks.

"In the valley of the Fayum to the south, we have a vast infertile basin. If that were connected to the Great River, it would open a large tract of land for agriculture. We could hire the poor to till it. It would raise our grain production by at least a tenth. Have I your permission to build a canal?"

Pharaoh sighed. "Of course," he replied carelessly. "You have the signet ring. Do what you like. You needn't bother to ask me in the future. I leave all these matters in your hands. Do as your God directs."

Joseph stared at the Pharaoh. The Grain Administrator's power was greater than he had imagined. Sutekh was not fully aware of just how great. Perhaps not even the Vizier Enkhu understood. When the seven years of famine came upon them, Joseph would be virtual ruler of Egypt.

"This completes my report, Lord Pharaoh." There was more, much more, but it was all details and statistics. His summary was all the Pharaoh cared about. If the dream interpretation were correct—and Joseph was convinced it was—the project was indeed on schedule and would be overwhelming successful. The whole world would turn to Egypt and bow before this Pharaoh.

Here Joseph was struck by a thought which almost staggered him. The power would be his. Not Pharaoh Sutekh's. Not Vizier Enkhu's. His. His alone. He would rule the world.

No. No. He shook his head, unaware of the Pharaoh's intense gaze. He would not accept such power. He was not the appointed ruler of the world. He was a servant. A servant of the Pharaoh. A servant of God.

He must be careful not to lose his perspective. How easy it would be for him to seek power, to revel in the luxury of control, to hold his head high as the most powerful man in the world.

It must not be. He was God's servant. *God,* not Joseph, was sovereign. God alone. Joseph resolved to remind himself of this every morning, when he offered his daily prayer to God. He must not lose this perspective.

Pharaoh Sutekh leaned back in his cushioned chair. "You have done well, Zaphenath-paneah. God is surely with you."

Joseph nodded. He must never take this compliment the wrong way, although he knew it was true. God *was* with him. He resolved always to give God the credit for his remarkable success.

Pharaoh's next words surprised him. "Zaphenath-paneah, it is time for you to marry."

Joseph was completely unprepared for this. At thirty-one years of age, he had adjusted to bachelorhood. Although his young healthy body had all the sexual fire and fury of a normal male human, he had suppressed it so successfully with the help of God and a lot of hard work that he now felt no need for a wife. But Pharaoh's word was law.

"It shall be as you say, my lord Pharaoh."

Sutekh smiled. He obviously enjoyed this role, believing he had a god-given power to create families. "Your wife shall be Asenath, the lovely daughter of Potiphera, priest of Hieropolis."

Joseph gasped. He had heard of Potiphera, although he did not know about his daughter. This priest was one of the most powerful men in the land. A Seth worshiper, of course, and in fact its high priest. Potiphera was thus very close to the Pharaoh. To be married to his daughter would connect him with powerful religious circles in Egypt.

Then Joseph understood. This was a political marriage. Although he tried to keep himself free of Egyptian politics, he had quickly discovered that it was impossible in his position as Grain Administrator. There were deals to be made, important personages to cultivate, manipulations and schemes and intrigue.

A sordid business, but it was business. There was no avoiding it. Joseph had conducted all his affairs as honestly and openly as possible and had gained the respect of even the most experienced politicians in Egypt.

Nevertheless, he must play the game.

The marriage into the family of the priest of Hieropolis would give him a tremendous advantage. It meant doors would open for him which were closed before. Instantly a whole priesthood of influential politicians would side with him. He could. . . .

Abruptly he shut off this train of thought.

Joseph stroked his chin. Marriage! His mind turned to the girl he would be marrying. "Lovely" was the word the Pharaoh had used to describe her. What did *that* mean?

Pharaoh had been smiling indulgently at Joseph's preoccupied look. He allowed him a moment of fancy, then brought him back to the present. "Let your steward make the arrangements. The marriage will take place in our large audience hall in one month."

"It shall be as you say, lord Pharaoh."

The audience was over. Joseph bowed and backed out of Pharaoh's presence. He left the royal residence and went to the far end of the palatial city where he kept his own residence and office. Joseph slept and worked in a small apartment, but it would not be suitable for a bride.

He called for his steward.

One of the first things Pharaoh had done after appointing Joseph Grain Administrator was to assign Buba as Joseph's personal steward. Joseph was pleased. Buba as chief cupbearer to Pharaoh had had much experience in managing the Pharaoh's household. He knew many people, and everybody knew him. He was able to do all the domestic things necessary for Joseph, so the Grain Administrator could turn to business without the bother of setting up a household.

The apartment where Joseph lived was full of cats, but it was well furnished and comfortable. The household staff which Buba had assembled were experienced and well trained. Buba was a valuable person to have around, and Joseph was grateful to him.

When Buba appeared, Joseph explained the Pharaoh's decree for his forthcoming marriage. Buba clapped his hands and grinned.

"Ah, the lovely Asenath. Bastet be praised, Joseph! What a remarkable marriage this will be!"

Again the use of the word "lovely" to describe his bride-to-be. Joseph looked forward to meeting this girl.

"There's a lot to do, Buba. I'll need a new place to live that will be more suitable for my new household. The wedding is to take place in one month. The Pharaoh has appointed you to be in charge of arrangements. Can you handle all that?"

It was a foolish question, and Joseph was instantly sorry he had asked it. For all his pomposity and loquacity, Buba was a capable steward. He could easily handle this assignment.

He would not have known it by Buba's reaction.

"The first thing I shall do, Joseph, is name a cat for Asenath. Yes, yes. It shall be a white angora. That will be just right for her. Then Bastet will be able to watch over her. Ah, the lovely Asenath! It shall be a pleasure to serve her. Thank you, Bastet, you are kind!"

Joseph smiled at his steward. He seemed so innocent, so silly, so detached from the world. Maybe the pose was deliberate. Joseph knew by now of Buba's competence and intelligence, but his manner was contradictory.

"Do as you think best, Buba. I leave it all to you."

After Buba left, Joseph frowned. He must turn his mind away from his forthcoming marriage. Several of his young assistants were waiting for him in his office, and he must commission two new grain silos today. The Fayum basin project must be set in motion. He had too much to do to think about weddings, moving, and lovely brides.

But he must not forget his promise to God. He must not reach for too much power.

10

The wedding was brief, even by Egyptian standards. Rarely did the Pharaoh Sutekh attend a social function, and when he did he always left early. When he left, the real party would begin. Sutekh frowned on the drunken orgies which characterized the usual Egyptian party.

Joseph had never seen his bride before that day. When she appeared at the wedding party with her parents, she was unfortunate in being placed beside the proud Queen Apopha. The queen's fabled beauty (or so she proclaimed, and no one dared deny it) outshone everyone in the kingdom, and (so she said) in the world. At that moment she outshone Asenath.

Part of Queen Apopha's fabled beauty was the unspoken law that no one in the kingdom dared wear anything which would upstage her. Asenath's parents were careful to subdue their daughter's taste in clothes when the queen would be present.

The queen wore a crown of royal blue, almost a foot high. Asenath's wig was not only several inches shorter, but not as bright a shade of blue.

The queen's face was as beautiful as the legends said. The smooth skin was highlighted only slightly by her makeup. Her lips reddened and cheeks pinked with rouge, her eyes in blue shadows, her eyebrows painted in royal blue, she was a classic beauty.

In contrast, Asenath seemed an undeveloped child. Her skin was pale. Under her blue wig, her forehead was short. Her eyes were petite and narrow, her cheeks pinched, her nose stubby, and her mouth small and thin. She looked so childish that Joseph wondered if she were more than fourteen or fifteen. She could not have reached puberty many years ago.

The queen's pectoral breastplate was striking. Basically gold, it was studded with carnelian, lapis lazuli, turquoise, amethyst, and garnet. In the center was a small design in blue and gold, representing the royal crest of the god Seth. Beside her, Asenath's pectoral breastplate looked plain, even though it was basic gold with blue lapis lazuli in filigree around it. There was no crest.

Queen Apopha wore a very becoming kalasaris. The flowing sleeves draped luxuriously over her arms and were gathered just above her wrists. The long skirt, white and pleated, reached to the floor slightly splayed, revealing her golden slippers. Asenath's kalasaris was unpleated and plain, with shorter sleeves. She looked quite ordinary compared to the dazzling Apopha.

Egyptian wedding ceremonies were short and secular. When the couple broke the ceremonial bridal jar, the groom spoke a few ritual words claiming the bride as his "sister."

Very briefly she answered in a subdued voice that he was her "brother." Although the Egyptian terms were familiar to Joseph, he had been raised to think of brother and sister as being blood relations, siblings of the same parents. He wondered if this was why he looked on his bride more as a little sister than a wife.

As she spoke the words claiming him as her "brother," she gazed up at him with a puppy look, reminding him of the way his slave Kali looked at him. Joseph understood. He was twice her age. She saw him as an adult, and she only a child. He was Zaphenath-paneah, bearer of the Pharaoh's signet ring. He must appear as much a big brother to her as she seemed a little sister to him. He wondered what difference this would make in the marriage bed.

Although he sat beside her during the banquet, he had no opportunity to talk with her. The orchestra played and the dancers gyrated, but everybody followed the Pharaoh's lead by refraining from conversation. Pharaoh was obviously bored, preferring to be with his soldiers watching a pair of swordsmen match skills. It was a relief to all when Pharaoh rose to leave, signifying that as far as he was concerned the party was over.

After the royal couple departed, the party loosened up. When the time came to escort the bridal couple to their chambers, most of the guests were becoming uninhibited. Buba had arranged for a luxurious residence for Joseph within the royal palace grounds. It was far more magnificent and spacious than his former spartan apartment, although he retained his former quarters as his business office.

Standing outside the large double doors of his new home, Joseph and his bride bade the revelers good night.

There were ribald jokes and comments, but Buba firmly shut the door and locked it. He then ushered Joseph and his new wife to their bedroom. Lamps had been lit. Buba closed the door after bidding them a wordy good night and commending them to Bastet.

The bride and groom were alone for the first time.

Joseph hesitated, embarrassed. He didn't know how to approach her in this awkward moment. As husband? As big brother? But Asenath solved the problem.

"Help me get out of this horrid dress!"

Her words took Joseph completely by surprise. He had been in Egypt for almost fourteen years and had been exposed again and again to Egyptians' casual attitude toward nudity in a hot climate. But he had been raised as a proper son of Israel and had never quite become accustomed to the sight of a bared female body.

Then a new thought struck him. This was not only the voice of an Egyptian who spoke to him, but the voice of a child. Most children in Egypt wore very little clothing. Only in public did they even bother to put on anything at all. Their childhood playmates of both sexes were almost always nude. Asenath was still a child in many ways, and probably was not at all self-conscious about clothing.

But she was his wife. As a "proper son of Israel" he had been taught that in intimate husband-wife situations nudity was not improper. And so he began to work on the clasp which held her pectoral breastplate in place.

She snatched off her wig and threw it on the floor. "That horrid wig!" She sniffed. "It's so hot!"

Joseph wondered if "horrid" were her favorite word.

He removed the breastplate and was shocked as she wriggled out of the kalasaris and dropped it on the floor. She stood before him completely naked.

He began to feel the stirrings of manhood which he had so successfully repressed during all of his adult life. His familiar discipline asserted itself and he turned his eyes away. But then he checked himself. She was his wife. He had every right to look at her. He did.

She was no child. At least as far as her body was concerned. What he saw was not opulence but the promise of opulence. The sight was breathtaking, and the word people were saying about her popped into his mind—*lovely*.

But she was not aroused like Joseph was. To her, the shedding of clothes was the natural thing to do now that the party was over. She wanted to talk.

"Tell me, my husband," she said shyly. "What shall I call you? Zaphenath-paneah is a horrid name. Isn't there something else I can call you? I'm your wife and I don't even know your name!"

"Has no one ever told you? My name is Joseph. The 'horrid Zaphenath-paneah' is the official name the Pharaoh gave me. Call me Joseph."

"Jo-seph. I am not familiar with that name. Is it foreign?"

"Yes. Didn't you know? I'm an Israelite from the land of Canaan. I came here fourteen years ago as a slave."

She gasped, and her eyes widened in horror. "You? A Canaanite? A slave?" She gaped at him.

Joseph had always known about most Egyptians' condescending attitude toward foreigners, especially Canaanites. Most Egyptians tolerated the foreigners they had conquered. But even after several generations they were still foreigners. In the Egyptians' opinion, foreigners were fit for nothing but slaves.

Joseph had been treated well during his years of slavery and was never exposed to the cruelty and degradation customary in Egypt. Nevertheless, he was a Canaanite. A foreigner.

It was a delicate moment. Joseph realized it could damage their relationship just as they were starting out. What should he say to reassure her?

"Think of me as a slave," he said gently. "I will serve you as an obedient slave should."

It was the right thing to say. An impish look appeared on her child-face; the corners of her mouth turned up. Her eyes crinkled in roguish delight.

"A slave! My husband is my slave!" She fairly bubbled with puckish pleasure. "You were born with sand between your toes! The great Zaphenath-paneah, Grain Administrator of all Egypt, second only to the Pharaoh in all the land—my slave. How fantastic!"

Joseph smiled. He was charmed by the elfin spirit he saw before him. She was not subdued in his presence now, not overawed at having married a peer of the realm. It would be good for their relationship for her to think of him as a slave, born "with sand between his toes" as she so quaintly put it. It brought him down to her level. Now he could be "husband" rather than "big brother."

"Slave!" She drew herself up haughtily. "My first order to you is: *Take off that horrid signet ring!*"

Joseph breathed a sigh of relief. There was something symbolic about this, her first order to her "slave." As he carefully placed the ring in the treasure box, he became aware of the change in her. She was no longer afraid of him. In her eyes he had been transformed from the great Zaphenath-paneah, Grain Administrator of Egypt, wearer of the powerful signet ring, into Joseph, her husband. She could now be his wife.

But more surprises were ahead for Joseph. He was to discover that his new wife not only had a very casual approach to nudity, but also had no inhibitions whatever about sex. "Now slave!" she said imperiously. "Take off your clothes!"

She laughed as he hurriedly undressed. She was so charmingly disarming, so naive and innocent, that he warmed to her. He wanted her physically but he enjoyed her youthful exuberance. He thought he would be able to love her, in the old-fashioned sense of that word.

11

The Great River was the aorta of Egypt. It brought to that nation its lifeblood. This aorta began hundreds of miles away in central Africa. Each year the heavy rains fell on the prairies and uplands around the great lakes. All the minor rivers flowed, like obedient blood vessels, into the Great River. It rushed north at tumultuous pace, plunging breathlessly through canyons and gorges until it spilled out onto the Black Lands of Egypt.

The Black Lands were so named by the ancient Egyptians because of the soil which the overflowing aorta deposited during flood stage. It was a strip about ten miles wide, wondrously fertile, contrasting with the Red Lands around it, untouched by the flood and therefore barren. The annual flood happened in late summer, and each year the dying land was bathed, enriched, and revitalized by the vibrant pulse of its mighty aorta, the Great River.

Each year the Egyptians depended on it. Once in a long time, it let them down. The rains in central Africa were light, and the flood stage was low. Then the Egyptians wrung their hands, bewailed their bad luck, and prayed to every god they had ever heard of. The gods would seem to combine their power, the next year the Great River would flood, and the people would again become happy and complacent.

Never had the Great River let them down more than

one year in a row. If it had, history would have remembered the resulting calamity forever. The Great River rolled on and on, occasionally skipping a year as though to remind them of its power, but always graciously renewing itself the following year.

In the eighth year following Joseph's assumption of office, the Great River let the people down. Drought devastated central Africa. The annual flood stage in Egypt was low, too low for crops. The people, as usual, wrung their hands, prayed to gods, and turned to the government for help. It happened in both the upper and lower kingdoms.

Joseph then opened the warehouses and distributed the grain. He did so judiciously, selling it dearly to the rich, giving it free to the poor. Unlike previous failures of the Great River, there was no hardship this year.

But it happened again the next year. This was unprecedented in Egyptian history. Again the wringing of hands and crying to gods, and once again all Egypt—north and south—turned to the government for help.

Suddenly Joseph had become the most powerful man in Egypt, more powerful than the Vizier Enkhu. The economic power in his hands far surpassed the political power of any other administrator. In Joseph rested the life and death of all the people of Egypt.

The ways of nature are strangely interrelated. When calamity struck in one place, there was tragedy in another. For some strange ecological reason, the rains failed in Canaan that year too. A severe drought caused the already meager grassland to turn dry and barren. Animals died, and people found it more and more difficult to live comfortably. The first year was hardship; the second year was disaster.

At the end of the second year of drought in Canaan, Jacob called his sons together. He was an old man, grayhaired and wrinkled, but as alert as any of his children.

Perhaps more so, because he had a native intelligence which had been matched by only one child, and that one had died tragically at age seventeen.

"The sheep are dying, Father." Judah stood before the old man, giving a report which was becoming all too familiar. He had replaced his brother Reuben as the leader of the brothers. "The goats are doing well enough, but they get so little to eat that even they are weakening. If this drought continues, we'll lose all our flocks."

Jacob glowered at Judah. "It's more than the flocks," he muttered. "It's our families. God is punishing us for some reason. We've got to do something."

Judah shook his head. "Father, my sons Er and Onan died as a result of my sins. I admit it. But that has nothing to do with this drought."

Jacob said nothing. Discussing theology would not solve the situation. He had a lot more to say to his sons on that subject, but this was not the time.

Reuben had been standing by the door while Judah reported. He now spoke, perhaps trying to assert his former leadership. "There is grain in Egypt. The caravans returning from the south are laden with it. It's expensive, but it may be our salvation."

There followed a general discussion of the situation in Egypt, as the brothers brought together everything they had heard from passing caravans. Mostly the talk was of one man, the Grain Administrator with an unpronounceable name, the most powerful man in Egypt. He and he only could dispense the grain they needed.

Jacob hated to let them go. His sons were full of ambition and wanderlust, wanting to travel to the fabled land to the south they had never seen. They could not travel east because of an ancient treaty Jacob had once made with Laban, but there was no reason they could not go to Egypt. Now they had to, and the men were eager to go.

Jacob wanted to send three of them, but they all wanted to see Egypt. Even Benjamin, the youngest, wanted to go. But Jacob was adamant. He had lost one favorite son; he would not risk losing another.

Finally they reached a decision. All ten of the brothers would go to Egypt to buy grain. Benjamin would remain at home with his father. There were plenty of servants to care for the flocks and herds while the brothers were gone. Jacob had enough silver in his treasure chest to buy what they needed, no matter what the price.

In the beginning of the third year of the drought, the brothers arrived in Egypt. They gaped and gawked at the sights. The Great River was like an ocean to them. The gleaming cities of Egypt, overpopulated and bustling, amazed them. The marble statues and temples and granite houses astonished them. The refinement of the linen-clad hairless people dumbfounded them. The exposed flesh of shameless women shocked them. By the time they arrived at Avaris, their senses had been so bombarded with new wonders they could barely appreciate that splendid city.

Eventually they came to the royal palace where the great Grain Administrator, Zaphenath-paneah, ruled. As they entered the palace gates, they thought they had come into another self-contained city. It was divided into four sections. They passed the temple area, aghast at the magnificent structure which dominated the neighborhood. The worker's village was larger than any of the cities of Canaan. They could see the royal residences, where it was whispered the Queen Mother lived, the most beautiful woman in the world who allegedly spent more time in other men's beds than she did in her husband's.

They came at last to the section where there were apartments and offices for important officials of the kingdom. Here they were ushered into the awesome presence of the great Grain Administrator.

12

Joseph sat at a table on the dais in his audience hall. Each morning he worked there, and the affairs of the kingdom engulfed him. In the third year of the famine, the business daily before him was the selling of grain to foreign emissaries. He had organized the distribution to the inhabitants of Egypt during the first year of the drought, and things ran smoothly now. The requests for food which Joseph dealt with now were from foreign delegations from outside Egypt.

They came from everywhere these days. From the land of the Mitanni, from the Hittites, from Syria, even from Babylon. Before him appeared Canaanites, Edomites, Ammoru. People who spoke strange languages and had unusual customs. And they all wanted one thing: grain.

Joseph's wonder had grown with the passing years. The power which rested in his hands had rapidly expanded. Egypt's empire had been divided since the invasion of the Shepherd-kings. While the southern kingdom paid tribute to the Shepherd-kings in the north, they were either fighting or smoldering with resentment against their northern neighbors.

But no more. The famine changed everything. The southern kingdom meekly paid tribute and begged for grain. The nations of the world also paid their tribute to Egypt, and regimes and tribes who once paid tribute to other Shepherd-kings now came to Egypt and humbly begged for grain.

Pharaoh's empire was strong again, not because of the chariots and bronze weapons, or the cunning of the vizier Enkhu. The empire was great solely because of the ingenuity and economic power wielded by the Grain Administrator. In his hands was the key to world sovereignty.

Another delegation was scheduled to come before him this morning, this one from Canaan. Another group of emissaries with their wiles and strategems—some begging, some demanding, some cajoling, some offering bribes. No two alike. Yet they were all the same, all in desperate need for something only Joseph could supply.

Before this delegation appeared, Joseph offered his now-familiar prayer. The power was God's, not his. He was the servant. None of this was his doing. He submitted himself before his only true Sovereign and pledged once again to serve his Lord. Now he was ready to receive the next group of people who came begging for grain.

The ten foreign emissaries came into the room, and for the first time Joseph looked up and saw them.

He gasped.

Half rising from his chair, he clutched the table before him. His head swam. He stared. He couldn't breathe.

Several moments passed while Joseph struggled to bring himself under control. The scribe who sat before him stared at Joseph with deep concern. The translators were startled. The bearded emissaries from Canaan had never seen the great Grain Administrator and seemed unaware that anything was amiss. But all of Joseph's assistants and business associates were in turmoil. Something was wrong with Lord Zaphenath-paneah.

Joseph took a deep breath and regained control of himself. He looked at his brothers. There was Reuben, old now, his beard streaked with gray. Judah looked more confident and self-assured. Simeon did not look as fierce as he had twenty-three years ago.

Twenty-three years! It seemed such a short time ago that he had heard Simeon's voice in the darkness. "My blade thirsts for his blood!" Or Judah bargaining with the Ishmaelite. Or Reuben cautioning him about telling his brother his dreams.

His dreams! They came back to him like the flood of the Great River in good times. The brothers were now making their obeisance to him, kneeling as they had been instructed by Buba, stretching out their arms at knee level. Just like in his dreams! His brothers were bowing before him.

Should he tell them now? Should he reveal who he really was? The words rushed to his tongue but were bitten back. No! The memories of their cruelties to him so many years ago were still fresh. Let them suffer! Suffer, the way they had made him suffer so many years ago.

And then he remembered his prayer, which he had offered to God just a moment ago. His prayer for humility, for perspective. He was God's servant, not placed here to exact revenge. He must not use God's power for personal ends.

He would question his brothers. He must know if they were the same bitter men who hated him so much they sold him into slavery. God had done so much for him. What had God done for them? He must find out.

He called for his Canaanite interpreter. His first question to his brothers surprised the interpreter.

"Where are you from?"

The hoarseness in his voice sounded ominous to the brothers. They did not suspect that it came from his barely controlled emotions.

Judah—not Reuben!—answered. "Sir, we are from the land of Canaan. We wish to buy grain."

Joseph understood immediately the familiar tongue,

but he waited patiently while the interpreter tra
gave him the minute he needed to plan what he
The time for testing had come.

He made his voice deliberately harsh. "No! you are spies! You are plotting against our nation!"

When the surprised interpreter translated this, the brothers looked at each other in dismay. Judah spoke.

"No sir. We are not spies. We have come to buy food. We are brothers. We are honest men. Please believe us, sir; we're not spies!"

"You *are* spies!" Joseph almost shouted the accusation. The brothers cringed. "You have come to spy out our weakness!"

Joseph watched as Judah collected himself and stood up tall before these cruel words.

"Sir," he said boldly, "we are *not* spies. We are only twelve brothers, and our father is in the land of Canaan."

Twelve brothers! It struck Joseph like a blow. In the minute he had between translation, he once again had to gain control of his emotions. Again his voice was hoarse when he replied.

"You are *ten* brothers. Do you think I can't count?"

"Sir, we are twelve brothers. Our youngest is at home with our father, and one of our brothers is dead."

Joseph was silent for a minute, absorbing this. Not just that they believed him dead, but that they still counted him as one of them!

"And your mother? Did you all come from the same womb?"

"No, sir. Our father had two wives and two concubines. Six of us were borne by the first wife. The concubines each gave him two sons, and his beloved wife gave him two."

"And do the mothers live?"

"Sir," he replied, "all are dead save one concubine, Zilpah, and she is old and feeble."

The news made Joseph lean back and catch his breath. Not only his mother but Leah was dead. The many changes made him sad. But he must not show his emotion openly now. What should he do? He needed time to think.

"This proves nothing," he thundered. "You are spies! And I tell you in the name of Pharaoh, you will not leave Egypt until your youngest brother comes here and stands before me! One of you may go to get him and bring him here, and the rest of you will be bound and put in prison.

"Then we'll find out if your story is true! If it turns out you have no younger brother, I will know you are spies. I will deal with you accordingly!"

The brothers quailed. Joseph barked quick orders; instantly they were surrounded by Egyptian soldiers. Despite their protests, they were bound and led away.

Joseph could do little work in the next two days. His thoughts were constantly on these new developments. What should he do? Had the brothers changed? He felt he had to know, so he determined to follow through with his plan.

On the third day he sent for them. They came back into his presence and bowed before him, stretching out their hands at knee level. Again Joseph remembered his childhood dreams.

He was ready now to talk to them. He had completely mastered his feelings. The harshness in his voice was not deep emotion but an act.

"I am a merciful man," he began, "and I am going to be gracious to you. I shall find out if you are spies or not. Only one of you will remain here. The rest of you will return to your home in Canaan, but you must return with your youngest brother. If all you have told me is true, I will spare you. If you don't return, the one who remains will die a horrible death!"

The brothers looked at each other, fear written on their

faces. Then Reuben turned to his brothers and spoke.

"It's true, like I told you years ago. All this is happening because you wouldn't listen to me but went ahead and murdered him, sending him into slavery!"

They spoke among themselves, unaware that Joseph could understand them.

"It's *my* fault," said Judah. "I should never have allowed him to be sold to the Ishmaelite! This is God's punishment for what I did!"

It seemed to Joseph that he had come into the middle of a discussion which had probably begun while they were together in the prison. But he got another surprise when the once volatile Simeon spoke.

"It was mostly my fault. I was young then. I wanted his blood. If there is any blame, it should fall on me. I should be the one who has to stay."

In spite of his determination to be strong, a rush of emotion flooded Joseph. Abruptly he stood and walked from the room. On a small balcony overlooking the Great River, he stood alone, and the tears rolled down his cheeks.

He now knew what he wanted to know. Should he tell them now? No. He would like to see his younger brother first. After a moment he took several deep breaths, dried his tears, and returned to the audience room.

The brothers were ready for him. To his surprise, Simeon stood forward. "Sir," he said, "I will stay and be your hostage. Let my brothers go."

"So let it be."

Joseph then turned the negotiations over to the assistant scribe and left the room. While the scribe collected their money and arranged for their grain sacks to be filled, Joseph called Buba and explained what he wanted done.

He gave orders for the silver which the brothers paid for their grain to be secretly returned. It was to be placed in their grain sacks, and cleverly concealed so they would not discover it until they arrived home.

He wondered what his father's reaction would be. He thought he knew. Honest Jacob would be instantly contrite. He would feel the money must be returned. But to do that he would have to send the brothers back with the youngest son. Would he do it? Of course he would! He wanted to see Simeon again alive, and they would need more grain. He had to do it.

And of course Jacob trusted in God. He was Israel, "the one who wrestles with God." Perhaps it would cause him some anguish for a while, some further wrestling with his God. But Joseph knew that in the end the youngest son would come.

It was God's will. And God's will be done.

13

In Hebron, Jacob was disturbed. He sat at the entrance to his tent as his nine sons reported on their experience in Egypt.

"This Grain Administrator," he said thoughtfully, "is a strange man. Full of contradictions. You say he seemed savage and brutal at times?"

"Yes, Father." Judah as usual spoke for the brothers.

"And yet you say some of the things you told him distressed him?"

Judah nodded. "It seemed that way to us. At one time he even left the room. The other Egyptians there looked worried about him."

"And he questioned you repeatedly about your family?"

"He not only wanted to know about you and Benjamin, but also about your wives and concubines. The only way we can prove we are not spies is to bring Benjamin with us to show we are speaking the truth."

"Odd." Jacob ran his fingers through his gray beard. Egyptians, to his way of thinking, were strange people, but the thinking of this Grain Administrator eluded him. Why should he think they were spies? What could their small clan do to mighty Egypt? And how could the existence of a younger brother back home prove they were not spies? It was very peculiar.

The strangest thing was the matter of the money.

"And you say you found all the money you had paid for the grain in the grain sacks?"

"That's true, Father." Judah shook his head slowly. "We can't understand it. I'm sure we paid him. We counted it out to the last piece of silver. It must be a mistake."

"It was no mistake." Jacob's agile mind struggled with the problem. Something was wrong. Very wrong. He couldn't begin to comprehend what it was. At the very least, it was sinister.

"We must return the money. He must know we're honest people after all. Maybe that's what he wanted: to test our honesty. If you go back to Egypt with the money, he might believe you and release Simeon."

"Father, listen to me!" Judah's voice rose, his beard thrust forward. "We can't return to Egypt without Benjamin. You should have seen that man! We can't—no, we *shall* not return to Egypt without Benjamin!"

Jacob rose, reaching for a tent pole to support him. His eyes flashed with the old fire of youth.

"What are you trying to do to me?" he rasped. "First there was my beloved son Joseph. Now Simeon. Next you want to take Benjamin from me. Well, you won't do it!"

Jacob turned suddenly and walked into the tent. Judah could barely hear his final words, "Why can't I have some peace?"

Reuben pushed passed Judah and stood at the entrance to the tent. "I understand, Israel." His words were soft.

Jacob paused, then turned, staring at his oldest son. Reuben had always been the most thoughtful and understanding of the fierce sons. Even though his rightful position of leadership had been displaced by Judah, he held no ill feelings. On the contrary, as he grew older Reuben reached out to his father with sensitivity and compassion. Reuben's use of the name "Israel" rather than "Father" set him apart from the others. He understood Jacob's constant wrestling with God.

Reuben continued. "Let the boy go to Egypt, Father. I will be responsible for him. I won't come back without him. I'll leave my two sons here with you. If anything goes wrong, and Benjamin doesn't come home, you may take my two sons as your own."

Jacob pursed his lips. This was a generous offer. The family placed great pride in their sons, believing them to be their foothold on immortality. A father would die, but his sons would live. As long as there were descendants, the clan would continue. And with it the mysterious Promise, handed down through the generations, that some day this clan would be a mighty nation, and through them all nations would be blessed by God. Reuben's offer meant that if Benjamin were lost, his two sons would replace him.

Jacob vigorously shook his head. "No. My son Benjamin shall not go. He's the only one of Rachel's sons left. If anything happened to him, I would die!"

Jacob searched Reuben's face for a reaction. He had bluntly told his oldest son that one of Rachel's sons was worth two of Reuben's. Reuben bit his lip and chewed on his beard. Jacob lowered his eyes. The rebuff to his son's thoughtful offer was severe, but it couldn't be helped. What he had spoken was the truth. He could not afford to lose another of his beloved Rachel's sons.

The meeting broke up with nothing decided. They did nothing; just waited, hoping the drought would soon be over. But the famine dragged on.

A year passed. Jacob sadly watched the dwindling supply of the grain his sons had brought from Egypt. He saw no change in the severe drought. He saw his flocks decimated. He saw the pinched cheeks of the little children in his clan. Something would have to be done—soon.

They would have to go to Egypt again.

What price would he have to pay for more grain? It wasn't the money which bothered him. It was Benjamin.

He confronted Judah one day with the problem. Judah had been thinking about it too.

"We must go Father. There's no other way."

"But can't you go without Benjamin?"

"No, Father. The Grain Administrator meant what he said. We must bring the boy with us, or we're all lost."

"You should never have told him you had a younger brother at home."

They had been over this ground before. Judah's voice was patient. "We couldn't help it. He asked us. He wanted to know every detail about our family. We saw no harm at the time in being completely open and honest with him."

"Honesty is always best, my son."

This was a lesson Jacob had learned from experience. In fact, it was the reason his name had been changed from Jacob to Israel. It was a lesson learned in struggle. Even now Israel continued to wrestle with God.

Jacob continued. "We must put our trust in God. He has watched over us in the past. I know God has a great destiny for our clan. God made it clear to our ancestor Abraham, and I'm sure it was confirmed for me at both Bethel and Penuel. We must have faith."

Something of Jacob's deep struggle with God communicated itself to Judah. He spoke softly. "Be at peace, Father."

Judah put his hand on his father's shoulder. "Send the boy to Egypt with me. I'll guarantee his safety. We all will. It's the only way."

"I know, Judah."

For the past year, Jacob had been wrestling with this decision, and now it had become clear. "It has to be that way. There's nothing else we can do. But this time, load your donkeys with gifts. Return all that money which rightfully belongs to Egypt, and take more. Take the best our country has to offer: balm, honey, spices, myrrh, pistachio nuts, almonds. Give them all to this Grain Administrator."

There was a pause. Then Jacob sighed. When he spoke, the words were wrenched from his soul. "And take your brother also. May Almighty God go with you, and stand beside you as you deal with this strange Egyptian. May God bring about the release of Simeon, Benjamin . . . and all my sons. And if it is God's will that all perish, then so let it be."

Judah's hand tightened on his father's shoulder. He stared long and thoughtfully into his father's eyes. Finally he nodded.

"Yes, Israel," he muttered.

14

"Greetings in the name of Zaphenath-paneah, and welcome to the land of Pharaoh Sutekh."

The formal greeting, delivered through an interpreter, surprised the brothers at the gate of the royal palace. Obviously they were expected.

"You may remember me. I am Bastakheron, steward of the house of Zaphenath-paneah. My master has requested that you dine with him today at his personal residence. Please come this way."

The brothers were astounded. They had fully expected to do business with the stern Grain Administrator in his business offices. To be invited to dinner at the man's home was most unusual. Something was wrong.

The steward led them through the picturesque streets of the palace-city. They passed the royal temple, its vast magnificence towering over everything. There were small shops along the way, and date palms swayed gracefully above them. Everything was clean and bright. The stone and brick buildings were solid.

They came to the royal residences, and once again the brothers were dumbfounded. Here was an imposing grandeur surpassing everything else.

They entered the Grain Administrator's residence through porticoes with carvings and paintings of brilliant colors. Inside, they stood in a large outdoor courtyard of flowers and fountains and statues and palm trees. Through a trellis they caught a glimpse of the Great River shimmering in the morning sunlight. The steward led them to a comfortable room overlooking the river. Luxurious chairs and couches lined the brightly painted walls. Here the interpreter told them to wait until midday, when dinner would be served.

"Please, sir," Judah's voice reflected his fear and hesitancy. "Ask the steward if we may be permitted to return the money which was mistakenly put in our grain sacks on our trip here last year. We have no idea how this money came to us. We have brought it with us to return it, along with more money for additional grain."

After a pause for translation, the answer came back. "Have no fear. Your God must have put it there. The money you paid for your grain last year was duly received and registered. You owe us nothing."

The steward then bowed and left the room, leaving ten astonished men behind. They erupted in a babble of conversation, edged with tiny pinpoints of fear as they discussed their uncertain future.

But more surprises were to come. Suddenly through the door walked their brother Simeon!

"Brothers! I'm here. All is well!"

Excited, they embraced him, questions bubbling so rapidly that Simeon finally held up his hands.

"Let me tell my story!" The brothers grew quiet, listening. "I have been in prison for a year—but such a prison. I've never before lived in such luxury! Freedom to move around, good clothes to wear, good food to eat, even a slave to wait on my every need. I've been so spoiled with comfort and luxury, I don't know if I can ever go back to my old life of tents and wilderness and smelly goats!"

He said this laughing, but it brought gasps of amazement from his brothers. They were full of questions.

"Did you find out anything about the Grain Administrator?" asked Reuben.

"I can pronounce his name now. Zaphenath-paneah. He's the most powerful man in Egypt. Nobody could talk about him except my slave and he talked about him all the time. Only I couldn't understand a word of what he said." He laughed. "It's good to be able to talk to someone again who understands what I'm saying!"

The morning passed rapidly. Their joyful reunion almost made them forget their desperate plight. The noon hour arrived, and with it the steward and interpreter to announce that dinner was ready.

They were escorted through imposing corridors brightly decorated with tapestries and pictures of flowers and people, until they came into a large airy room with a fountain and pool in the center. Tables were set up in three sections. One was a high table, with one place setting. The other two tables were set for eleven and sixteen. The steward led them to the one set for eleven. A clean white linen cloth, festooned with fruit and flowers, covered the table.

The steward and the interpreter had a list for the seating. The brothers gaped as the interpreter began to read their names—in order of age!

"Reuben." The steward pointed to the first chair. Reuben, shaking his head in awe, stood behind it. "Simeon." The next chair. "Levi . . . Judah. . . ." And so on, until finally Benjamin was pointed to a chair.

The table had been cunningly arranged, with Benjamin's place closest to the head table. The brothers didn't know what to make of this and buzzed with astonishment as they tried to figure out how he even knew their names. Of course, the names would be in the record of the grain recipients, but why go to all that trouble?

They noticed then several Egyptian noblemen standing at the other table, looking haughtily at the foreign intruders. Slaves stationed around the walls with ostrich fans created a breeze in the room. The fountains, sweet-smelling flowers, clean surroundings, and flowing fresh air made it a wonderfully pleasant dining room.

The Grain Administrator appeared and went to the dais table at the head of the room. The Egyptian noblemen bowed respectfully, and the brothers did the same.

Judah spoke through the interpreter. "Sir, we have brought gifts for you. May we present them to you now?"

The Grain Administrator nodded. Several slaves went to bring in their gifts. For best effect, the brothers presented them one at a time. First the balm, then the honey, followed by the nuts and spices. When the presentations were completed, the great man smiled. "Thank you," he said.

It was a good start. The brothers relaxed. But the man at the head table would not be seated. He was not yet ready to eat. "Welcome back to Egypt," he said through the interpreter. "And how is your father, the old man you told me about on your last visit?"

"He is well," Judah answered, surprised at this, not only that he would remember them in such fine detail, but also that he would care about their father back home. What had happened to the stern official who accused them of being spies last year? Judah shifted uneasily before this uncharacteristic cordiality.

The Grain Administrator stared at them. His stare was concentrated on Benjamin. "Is this your youngest brother, the one you told me about?"

"It is, sir."

"Welcome to Egypt, young man. May God be gracious to you."

Abruptly the Grain Administrator turned and walked out of the room. The Egyptian noblemen at the other table seemed just as startled at this as the brothers.

A few moments later the man returned. As yet, no one had seated himself at the table. Egyptian custom required that the host be seated first. The Grain Administrator went directly to the head table, sat down, and began to eat. At this signal, everyone took a seat.

Then began a meal such as the brothers had never dreamed was possible. A retinue of slaves entered the room, carrying trays with enough food to feed three armies. Wine glasses were filled first. When the brothers hesitantly sipped it, they discovered it was the finest beverage they had ever tasted: light and fragrant and sweet, and amazingly cool. Each time they placed their cup on the table, a slave stepped forward and filled it again.

Slaves served them four kinds of meat: beef, mutton, goose, and duck. Fortunately, no pork. The brothers sampled them all, finding them prepared to perfection with spices and gravies which enriched rather than spoiled their taste. Then came the vegetables in creamy sauces and fruits of many kinds. Four kinds of bread were placed around the table. An orchestra played soothing music in the background.

Unused to such a feast, they ate and drank too much. Their tongues were loosened and they began to relax and speak freely, unaware that the man at the head table could understand every word they said.

They enjoyed themselves so much, they failed to notice that the man seated alone at the end of the dining hall ate and drank little, but watched and listened to his guests with attentive eyes and ears. Occasionally he would beckon a slave and point to a morsel of food on his table. The slave would then place it on a silver platter and unobtrusively carry it over to the brothers' table, placing it near Benjamin's plate. The brothers took no notice of this, being too absorbed in eating and drinking and enjoying themselves.

Half way through the meal, Judah suddenly realized he was getting drunk. This would never do. He ceased eating and drinking, and struggled to clear his head. By the time the meal was over, he was the only sober man at his table.

Judah noticed that the man at the head table was sober also and was watching him. The ruler didn't look too imposing now. In spite of his immaculate wig, his clean shaven face, and that expensive-looking white linen garment, the man looked almost human. This contrasted sharply with his demeanor of last year.

Then again the Grain Administrator rose and left the room. The Egyptian noblemen at the other table were not surprised this time. Evidently it signaled the end of dinner.

The steward and interpreter appeared and led them to a suite of comfortable rooms overlooking the Great River. It was late afternoon; the brothers were glad to have an opportunity to rest and settle their stomachs, clear their heads, and sleep off the heavy drowsiness. They were a little ashamed of their excesses.

They arose at dawn, wondering what this day had in store for them. The steward and interpreter arrived at their room as if on schedule. "Your donkeys are loaded and ready to go," the steward told the brothers. "You may leave when you are ready. And I have a gift for you from myself, personally."

They had already noticed that he carried a cat in his arms—a beautiful gray and black cat, with sleek fur and pointed ears. The soft green eyes blinked lazily.

The steward went to Benjamin and handed it to him. Through the interpreter he said, "It's name is Benjamin. Bastet the great goddess will watch over you while this cat lives."

The boy Benjamin stroked the smooth fur and grinned. "Why, thank you, sir," he replied. "I shall take good care of it."

Judah stepped forward and motioned to the interpreter that he wanted to speak to the steward. "We are grateful for your hospitality, sir. Please convey our respects and appreciation to your master. Here is the money for the grain we have purchased."

He held out a large sack of silver. They had carefully counted and weighed it to the exact amount, including the money they found in their grain sacks last year.

The steward accepted it with a smile. "May Bastet go with you," he murmured.

"And may God richly bless you and your master!" Judah's benediction was sincere. Their visit this year had been much more pleasant than last year's.

15

They began their journey home along the now familiar road through the delta of the Great River. The day was hot, and their heads still ached from the unaccustomed revelry of the day before. Simeon especially suffered, having lived a whole year in luxury. He spent most of the day riding a donkey while the others walked.

They stopped early that evening and made camp. As they were eating their meager meal, a commotion arose at the edge of the camp. A group of horsemen rode in.

Judah sprang to his feet in alarm. Before him were soldiers, mounted cavalry, a small but highly trained part of Egypt's great army. Most Egyptian soldiers were either foot soldiers or charioteers, but this small elite band was known to all as one of the most highly skilled military squads in the world. Even the brothers had heard of them.

Then with a creaking of wheels and traces, a chariot drove up. In it, besides the driver, were the Grain Administrator's steward Bastakheron and the interpreter. These two men alighted from the chariot and strode toward the brothers.

"What have you done? It was a wicked thing to do!" Buba was bubbling with rage. The interpreter could hardly keep up with him. "You are evil wicked people, ungrateful to the kind benevolent man who treated you well while you were his guests.

"You are thieves! You are scoundrels! You are unworthy to own the cat I gave you! Shame on you, evil foreigners! May you feel Bastet's claws!"

"What are you saying?" Judah spread his hands. "We have done nothing wrong. We brought back the money we found in our grain sacks last year. We paid you for what we bought this year. What have we done?"

Buba stamped his foot. "By Bastet, you are evil! You have stolen a silver cup from my master's house! That's what you have done, ungrateful foreigners!"

The translator was working hard, but he managed to keep up with the flow of conversation.

"No, No! It can't be true!" Judah protested. "What kind of people do you think we are, to do something as terrible as that after the kindness you have shown us? Why should we steal anything from your master's house? We have what we came for, and we are most grateful!"

"Nevertheless," said Buba sternly, "a cup was missing from the very room in which you stayed. It was a valuable cup, made of pure silver and inlaid with gold. Who else but you could have stolen it?"

"But we didn't! Here, let me make you an offer," Judah plunged ahead recklessly, without thinking. "Search our belongings. If you find that we have stolen anything at all from your master's house, let the man who stole it die. The rest of us will be slaves forever to your master."

Although it was a bold challenge and spoken thoughtlessly, Judah was sure of his honesty. He knew he and his brothers were innocent.

"Fair enough," replied the steward, "except that there shall be no killing. The one who stole it will be a slave, and the rest of you may go free. Now let us search."

Each of the brothers spread out before the steward his own personal belongings, then opened the sacks of grain they carried.

"Nothing in mine," said Reuben.

"Nor mine," said Simeon, and the other brothers echoed him.

But Benjamin was silent. Fear descended on all the brothers. Benjamin held up the silver cup which he had found in his pack.

The next sound that broke the stillness of the night was the tearing of clothes. The brothers gave vent to their dismay and fear through the ancient custom of rending their garments.

"You will come with me, young man!" said Buba sternly.

"No! We will all come!" Judah's voice was strong. All the brothers supported him. It would be unthinkable for them to go on, leaving behind their youngest brother. They could never face their father without him. They would die first.

After traveling all night in company with the cavalry unit and the chariot carrying Buba and the interpreter, a weary and bewildered group of brothers arrived at the royal palace in the morning. They were taken directly to the Grain Administrator's office, and ushered immediately into the presence of the great man.

The audience room in the Grain Administrator's office was silent, charged with tension and anger. Before them on the dais stood the great Zaphenath-paneah, the most powerful man in Egypt. He towered above them, stern and vengeful. Armed soldiers were stationed around the walls.

The brothers were terrified. This was unreal, a nightmare from which they could not awake. They went down on their knees and stretched out trembling hands before the awesome power above them.

In the silence, only Judah's muttered prayer was heard. "God. We need you now!"

16

Joseph stood behind the table on the dais looking down on his kneeling brothers. He nodded. This was his last test.

He had ordered Buba to place the silver cup in Benjamin's pack. Then he had sent Buba with the soldiers to intercept the brothers, timing it so they would have to make an all-night return to the royal palace. Joseph had been anxiously waiting since dawn for their return.

Joseph looked down at his cowering brothers. He had led them deliberately to this moment. They had been lulled by good treatment since they arrived, then sent away with his good wishes. Now he had brought them back, exhausted and frightened, ready for the final test.

One thing he needed to know. Would they sacrifice Benjamin for their own safety? Twenty-four years ago, they had sold their father's favorite into slavery with no more compunction than they would sell a sheep. Would they do it again? Had they truly changed?

He made his voice harsh. "What have you done? Did you think you could get away with this? Don't you know who I am?"

The question was ambiguous, but he was the only one who knew that.

Judah rose to his feet. Joseph tried to look deeply into the soul of his brother. Something was happening to Judah. He seemed to be making a valiant effort to control his emotions. When he finally raised his head and looked Joseph in the eye, the fear was fading from his face. The set of the jaw, the thrust of the beard, the blaze in the eyes told Joseph that somewhere deep inside, Judah had found the strength he needed for this desperate moment.

When Judah finally spoke, his voice was steady. "Please, sir. Hear me out. I know you have in your hand the power of life or death over us. But we are innocent of the charge of theft. Our brother Benjamin did not steal that cup, nor did any of us. If one of us is guilty, we are all guilty. We have all returned for your justice."

His words were translated quickly. Joseph sternly gave his reply. "No! Only the one who stole the cup shall stay and be my slave. The rest of you may go!"

At these words, all the brothers rose to their feet and crowded around Benjamin.

Judah then stepped forward and stood at the foot of the dais steps. "Sir, please listen while I plead our cause. Last year when we were here, you asked us about our family. We told you then of our father and our youngest brother who is our father's favorite. This young man is the only remaining son of his beloved wife, Rachel, since the other boy was killed.

"Then you accused us of being spies! We are not spies, and we said so. But you demanded that we bring our youngest brother back to prove we spoke the truth. You kept our brother Simeon here as hostage until our return."

Judah's voice rose, becoming more confident as he continued. "Sir, we told our father this. He was dismayed. At first he would not let this happen. He said it would kill him if his only surviving favorite son were to leave. But the famine grew worse, Simeon was still a hostage, and our father bowed to the reality of the situation and let the boy come to Egypt with us."

Judah paused. He had been concentrating so hard on

his speech he had not noticed when the great man on the dais motioned to the interpreter to cease translating. It seemed only natural that he should continue.

"Sir, we can't go back without this boy. I myself pledged my life as a guarantee for his safety. So did Reuben. So also would every one of us. We would never consider going back to our father without him. It would kill him, and it would probably kill us. *We will not do it!*"

Judah's last words were thundered. The Egyptians in the room were startled, unable to understand what he was saying since the translator had fallen silent. But Judah wasn't through.

"If you must keep someone as your slave, take me! Or take any one of us, or all of us! *But let the boy return to his father!*"

"Enough!"

Joseph's word erupted with such vehemence that he forgot to speak in Egyptian. But in that highly charged moment, even the brothers failed to notice he had spoken in their own language.

Joseph's next words were in Egyptian. "Clear the room! I want everyone to leave immediately! *Everyone!*"

The Egyptians gasped. In the stunned silence, Buba jumped forward to obey his master. "Out! Out! All of you!"

He hustled around the room pointing people to the door. The soldiers and officials filed out of the room. Finally Buba closed the door behind him. Joseph was alone with his astonished brothers.

Judah and his brothers could see tears streaming down the cheeks of the great Grain Administrator. Then the mighty man, the most powerful man in Egypt, stumbled down the steps from the dais and stood before them.

"Brothers!"

The word was in their own language. It shocked them.

They still didn't know what was happening.

"I am your brother!"

They gaped at him in stunned silence.

"I am your brother!" he said again. "Your brother whom you sold into Egyptian slavery twenty-four years ago. God had watched over me, and has brought us all to this moment!"

The brothers looked at each other and then back to Joseph. They still couldn't comprehend what was happening.

"I am Joseph!" he said. Still they stared, mouths open. "God is good. God has been with me from the time I entered Egypt as a slave until this moment. God has sent you to me in time of famine and has great things in store for our family."

"Joseph?" Reuben recovered first from the shock, perhaps because he had less on his conscience than his brother. He stepped forward, and Joseph embraced him. Joseph could say no more.

The sight of the most powerful official in Egypt embracing their older brother shook the others out of their daze.

"Joseph! Is it possible? Is it really you?" They crowded around him, and he embraced each one in turn.

Simeon's embrace was hesitant. "Can you forgive me?" he sobbed.

Joseph again could not stop his tears. "I hold nothing against you," he murmured. "Don't be angry with yourselves about the past. Everything was done under the guiding hand of God. Even if you meant it for evil, God meant it for good."

Young Benjamin evoked the deepest emotion from Joseph. Short-bearded and wide-eyed, he stood open-mouthed before the brother whose mature face he had never seen.

"Joseph!" he finally stammered. "Is it really you? But

you can't be—you're dead. Or you were—but . . . but. . . ." Unable to say more, he clutched Joseph in his arms and wept.

Judah recovered first from the grip of the powerful emotion which held them all.

"My brother!" he said, smiling. "Father will be overjoyed to know you're alive and the most powerful man in Egypt!"

His words brought Joseph back to earth. He shook himself, throwing off the emotional shock which gripped him.

"You must return to our father," he said. "Bring him back to Egypt with you. I want to see him again. Move everybody here. You will be well taken care of. Always you will be under my protection."

Judah hesitantly laid his hand on Joseph's shoulder. He told himself that this was his brother, not Zaphenath-paneah, the great Grain Administrator of Egypt. He struggled with the awe that still held him.

"It shall be as you say, brother. It is God's will, and may God be praised!"

17

"Joseph! Joseph! Joseph!"

The word floating out of the valley reached Jacob's ears. He stood on the hillside near his permanent encampment at Hebron. Word had reached him about the approach of his sons—all eleven of them. With a muttered prayer of thanks, he had painfully climbed the hill to watch the road where they would come up through the valley.

He heard the chant, but he didn't understand it. "Joseph!" What did it mean? The brothers were shouting his dead son's name as they approached. They appeared to be in excellent spirits, full of enthusiasm and noise, their grain sacks filled to overflowing. They had several extra donkeys and even some wagons with them—more than they had when they started.

But why? What did it mean? "Joseph! Joseph! Joseph!" He could not mistake the name, the name of his dead son. Had they lost their senses?

His old eyes couldn't see as clearly as they once did, but he could see well enough to count them. Eleven. And their obvious good spirits meant all was well. One detached himself from the others and dashed up the hill. That would have to be Benjamin. Only the youngest would run uphill at the end of a long journey.

What was he saying? "Joseph is alive!" Had he gone mad? Joseph was dead, and had been for twenty-four years—no, almost twenty-five years now. What was wrong with this boy?

"Joseph . . . is alive!" the boy panted as he stumbled up the last slope and collapsed at Jacob's feet. "He's alive! He is . . . the Grain Administrator . . . of Egypt!"

"Be at ease, my son. Catch your breath, and then tell me. What's this nonsense you're babbling?"

Jacob was outwardly calm, but inside a heavy weight pushed down on his chest. His breath came in short gasps. It was almost as though Benjamin's breathlessness had been transferred to him.

"Father! It's true! Joseph is alive, in Egypt, and God has blessed him so wondrously he has risen to be second only to the Pharaoh. He's the Grain Administrator! He sends you his love and asks that we all come to Egypt to live with him!"

Jacob felt a weakness in his knees and a slight dizziness in his head. He sank down on a nearby rock. He still didn't comprehend with his mind what the boy was saying. His emotions were absorbing it first. His heart raced wildly, pounding as though it would burst in his chest.

"Joseph? What Joseph? Who is alive?"

"Joseph! My brother! Your son, whom you thought was dead. He didn't die, but was sold into Egypt as a slave. He's still there, alive and well, and sends you many gifts. God has blessed him amazingly!"

The message now swept past Jacob's emotions and into his mind. Joseph. His son who was dead. His first favorite, the first-born son of his beloved wife, Rachel. Alive! Could it be? Was it true? It must be! But how could it?

By that time the others had climbed the hill and stood around him. They all talked at once, but finally Judah quieted them with a word. "Father, you must go to your tent. The excitement is too much. You don't look well. Here, let me help you."

A few minutes later, in the cool shadows of the tent, Judah told the story. His telling was more restrained than Benjamin's. He told all, including the twenty-five year deception—of the favorite's robe soaked in goat's blood, of the selling of Joseph to the Ishmaelite for slavery in Egypt, of Joseph's subsequent rise to power.

By the time Judah had explained why Joseph withheld his identity from them for a full year to test them, the shadows of evening had fallen across the tent. The hearty aroma of a welcome-home feast pervaded the camp.

When Judah finally told his father that Joseph wanted the family to move to Egypt for the remainder of the famine, or even to live there always under his protection, Jacob wept. "It must be so, then," he murmured. "Joseph is alive. I will go to Egypt, and see my son before I die!"

Preparation for a permanent move called for great effort on everyone's part. For many weeks the entire clan busied themselves with inventories, gathering the scattered flocks and herds together, and organizing their traveling procedure. Carefully they packed the wagons Joseph had sent from Egypt. Their plans called for more than just a visit. This was a migration. Everybody and everything would go. Jacob set up his departure camp in Beersheba.

When all was ready, Jacob called his family together. They had built an altar of stone, and a large fire burned on it. Jacob carefully selected the largest bull he could find in his small herd of cattle. Then he chose twelve of his sheep and twelve of his goats, each one a perfect and healthy animal, not an easy task in those famine-ridden days. The bull would represent himself and the sheep and goats his sons.

He slit the animals' throats himself, and his sons skewered them and set them to roasting whole on the flaming altar. The smoke of the sacrifice billowed into the air, "The sweet smell of incense to the nostrils of God," as his father Isaac had poetically described it once.

Jacob turned from the altar, his clothes streaked with the blood of the sacrifice, and looked at his family. Fifty-five men stood before him. He had eleven sons, not counting Joseph in Egypt. He had thirty-nine grandsons and four great-grandsons. And wives and daughters. He gazed thoughtfully at the sight before him on the grassy slope before the altar.

Thirty-nine of the men and boys were descendants of Leah. Fifteen had descended from his concubine Zilpah, seven from his concubine Bilhah. That left only Benjamin from the womb of his beloved Rachel. But there was also Joseph in Egypt. He must get used to counting Joseph again. And Joseph, he was told, had an Egyptian wife. She already had one fine son, and was expecting another.

This was more than a clan. This was the beginning of a nation. This was the fulfillment of the Promise that through this nation all people would be blessed.

Jacob turned again and watched the smoke from the sacrifice curl up to the sky. "Thank you, God," he murmured. He felt a deep, overwhelming peace.

He recalled the time when he was young, when he had spent the night on a hard stone pillow, dreaming of the angels ascending and descending on a ladder from heaven. His life was like that. Up and down, up and down, with God . . . and apart from God. He had been Jacob then, Jacob the grasper, Jacob the supplanter, Jacob who had deceived his father and stolen his brother's birthright and had no peace.

He remembered that night at the fords of the Jabbok River when he had wrestled with the man he now knew was really God. That man had changed his name. He became Israel, "the God-wrestler." He had felt peace then, a new direction, but always he strove with God, with himself, with life.

He had known suffering, losing both wives and also his

favorite son. But he was Israel, and he knew that even in the valley of suffering, God was walking with him—even as he continued to wrestle.

Now something had changed. As he watched the smoke of the sacrifice ascend to God's nostrils, he felt a deeper peace. It was different now. He was going to Egypt, and God would go with him. He had with him a large family, the beginning of a great nation. Joseph lived in Egypt, waiting for him.

Was he now emerging from the valley of suffering to walk on the heights with God? There would be more conflicts ahead, for himself and his people. Suffering was inescapable in his life, especially for someone named "God-wrestler." But God would always be with him.

He was Israel, and these were his children. He turned from the altar and looked at them again. Their upturned faces were reverent as they quietly awaited his word.

He frowned as another thought struck him. Before him were his children, his family, who would always be known as the people of Israel. A difficult name to carry through the years. They would struggle and suffer too. But of course their striving would always be with God. No matter how much wrestling was ahead of them, God walked with them. That would be their peace.

"Shema!" he shouted. "Hear me, my children. The Lord our God—the Lord is God! He alone is our Lord!"

It may not have been the grandiose speech his family expected, but it touched something deep inside them. They were one, but not because their father was Israel. They were one because they were God's children. That was their reason for being.

With high hopes and a song of praise on their lips, they began the long migration to the land of Egypt. Behind them the smoke of the sacrifice rose like sweet incense to the nostrils of God.

18

"O king, live forever! May God lift up his countenance upon you, and give you peace!"

The large audience hall where Joseph met with his sovereign was now almost empty. Only two other persons were present: the cupbearer and scribe. More and more in recent years, the Pharaoh had elected to conduct his business in private. Now the fountain splashing water in the pool was almost thunderous.

Joseph's greeting and benediction to the Pharaoh were bold, since the Pharaoh was a worshiper of Seth. However, in recent years Joseph had often spoken openly about his God, and Pharaoh Sutekh had shown no sign of resentment. On the contrary, he had often shown signs of acceptance, as though Joseph's God were now the true God of Egypt. And why not? Had not Joseph's God done wonders for his country? To Pharaoh Sutekh, Joseph's God was real and powerful. And Joseph knew this.

"God has truly blessed us, Zaphenath-paneah." Sutekh's words reflected Joseph's thoughts, that the Pharaoh had accepted his God as at least equal to, if not greater than, Seth. "Your God leads you daily and works through you. As you know, this is not only a great privilege, but a burdensome responsibility. We are the ones through whom your powerful God works. And your God is surely at work throughout the whole of the earth."

The Pharaoh paused. "And how is God's work progressing through your hands, Joseph?"

Joseph unrolled a papyrus scroll. He gave a long progress report on the fifth year of the famine. Finally he was finished and laid aside the scroll.

"If it please you, sir, may I present to you my family?"

Pharaoh smiled and leaned back on his throne. "I have been looking forward to meeting them, ever since I learned they had arrived in Egypt. You may present them to me now."

Joseph spoke briefly to Pharaoh's cupbearer, who went to the other room to bring in his brothers. According to his plan, he would bring in his brothers first, then his father. He wanted the brothers to talk business with the Pharaoh, and his father to have a more relaxed conversation.

Five brothers strode into the room. He had chosen Judah, Reuben, Simeon, Levi, and Benjamin to represent his family. Their appearance contrasted strangely with the usual Egyptian looks. Their long hair and bearded faces, coarse woolen robes, sandals, and shepherd's staffs looked odd in this setting. Their weather-beaten faces were quite different from the refined soft skin of the Egyptians of Pharaoh's court.

The brothers were visibly impressed by the large audience hall and the presence of the Pharaoh. They went down on their knees and stretched out their hands at knee level. They noticed as they did so that the color of the blue floor was not just surface paint, but ingrained in the material. They had never seen anything like it.

Joseph told his brothers to rise. Then he presented them one at a time. Pharaoh gave his blessing to each, which Joseph translated. When he presented Benjamin, the Pharaoh said, "May your God smile upon you, young man, and give you many fine sons."

Benjamin grinned. He was the only one of the brothers

who was unmarried. He knew he must marry—and soon, to take his place among his brothers, all of whom had many children. He had his eye on one of his nieces and fully intended to make Pharaoh's benediction come true.

Pharaoh continued speaking, and Joseph translated. "What is your occupation?"

The brothers had been warned Pharaoh would ask this question. He had good reason to ask it, and Joseph had explained it to them. The Pharaoh's herds had increased during the past few years, and he needed shepherds and herdsmen to watch over them.

Judah replied. "We are shepherds, like our ancestors before us. We have not only sheep but cattle and goats and asses. We have come to Egypt with our flocks and herds because of the famine. We request your permission to settle in the land of Goshen."

The Pharaoh nodded. "Zaphenath-paneah, they are in your hands. Place them where you like. The land of Goshen would be good a place. And oh yes! If you see fit, let them be in charge of some of the royal livestock."

The last sentence was spoken carelessly, almost as an afterthought, but Joseph had discussed this with him several times in the past.

"It shall be as you say, my lord Pharaoh." After translating, Joseph turned back to the Pharaoh. "Now, if it please you sir, I would like you to meet my father."

The cupbearer left to bring in Jacob. Soon the old man walked into the room. That he was old was instantly obvious. His long gray hair and beard and wrinkled face proclaimed vast age. But his step was springy, his head held high. He could easily have gone to his knees before Pharaoh, but he chose not to. Instead, he bowed his head respectfully.

"May God richly bless you, Pharaoh Sutekh," he said as though speaking to an equal. "May God give you life and health and joy. For the vocation to which our God has called you, may God give you justice, mercy, and compassion."

Joseph translated faithfully, and Pharaoh seemed impressed. Joseph knew why. All his life he had been surrounded by inferiors, people who bowed submissively and fawned on him. For the first time in his life, he faced someone who treated him as a peer. Far from being offended by this, he was pleased.

"You are old!" Pharaoh's statement was not insulting, but respectful.

Jacob's reply lost nothing in the translation. "My years have been ones of hard work and struggle. I come from a long-lived race and have several years to go before reaching the age of some of my ancestors."

At this time, Pharaoh Sutekh was a comparatively young man, but he looked by far the older of the two. In spite of Jacob's long gray hair and beard and wrinkled skin, he was in better health than the younger Pharaoh. Sutekh's military interests were more administrative and executive than physically active. The life he lived was filled with rich food, strong wine, cushioned chairs, and concerns of the kingdom. This contrasted with the rugged outdoor life Jacob had lived, and it could be seen in the way the two men carried themselves.

The Pharaoh was interested in Jacob's faith. "Tell me about your God," he said.

As Joseph translated, he marveled at this strange request. Sutekh believed in Jacob's God because he had seen him at work in Joseph's life. But he also believed in Seth. Why, then, this line of questioning?

"God is one God, and there is no other!" Jacob fell easily into the old theological terms which had come down to him from his father and grandfather. "God created the world and made all things. In God's hand are the deep places of the earth; the strength of the hills is God's also. God be praised forever and ever!"

The Pharaoh nodded vigorously. "Amen!" he said.

The Egyptian equivalent for this word which Pharaoh spoke meant roughly, "It is true." Joseph frowned, puzzled. What was going on here? Was Sutekh considering adopting Jacob's God and turning away from his own? Or was he interested in establishing a twofold deity in Egypt?

The interview was over. Joseph quietly spoke to his father advising him to withdraw. But Jacob had one more thing to say.

"May God bless you, Pharaoh Sutekh." It was most unusual to give two benedictions in one interview. But Jacob wasn't finished. "I know of your strong faith in your god, as well as your acceptance of our God. I too have wrestled with heavenly visions. May God give you peace, even as God has given me peace."

As Joseph translated, he could see the deep respect Pharaoh accorded Jacob. A rapport existed between these two men that escaped the notice of everyone in the room except Joseph. The two understood each other. One was the sovereign of the greatest nation on earth. The other was a simple shepherd. Yet they faced each other as equals.

"Go in peace, my friend," said Sutekh.

Joseph blinked. This was probably the first time the Pharaoh had called any one friend. Only Joseph was aware of the great honor this bestowed on Jacob.

As Joseph bowed and took his leave, he was suddenly struck by something. The magnificent room, the panoply of royalty, the gold and silver and precious jewels—all faded into insignificance. On the throne sat a man—a lonely man. Pharaoh of the land of Egypt he might be, and the most powerful ruler in the entire world, but to Joseph at that moment he was just a man whose life was incomplete.

The Pharaoh lacked a God he could call friend. And he

had just met another man who had found a faith which gave him peace. For the first time in Sutekh's life, he had had a man-to-man confrontation with an equal, one whose faith gave him a royalty and regal bearing even greater than the Pharaoh's. This had left Sutekh, Joseph perceived, feeling empty.

As Joseph left the room, he smiled. Surely God was in this place today. God had brought together Israel, "he who struggles with God," and Sutekh, who was even now beginning to struggle with his faith. Perhaps God had spoken to him through this confrontation.

And if that were so, what did that mean for the future of Israel?

19

The four wands clattered on the floor. Asenath clapped her hands. "Four places!" she shrieked, moving her carved piece to a square on the board blocking Manasseh's next move. The game they played was senit. Joseph could not tell who displayed more childish glee: Asenath or their son Manasseh.

Manasseh was twenty years old, but with the youthful enthusiasm of a child. Just like his mother. She was now thirty-six, but still a child. Effervescent, bouncy, and still beautiful. She refused to change with the years.

Manasseh cast the wands on the floor, and shook his head ruefully. "I needed a four to get past you, Mother. But you're blocking me in the three square, so I can't go anywhere. Your turn."

Asenath's bubbling laugh filled the room. Joseph smiled contentedly as he leaned back on his cushioned chair. Last year he had retired from active government service and moved to Hieropolis to live with his wife's widowed mother. The famine had been over for several years, and Egypt still prospered. Hieropolis was just a few miles from Goshen where his family had settled and taken up their job as royal herdsmen.

For a while Joseph watched the game, but eventually his mind wandered. Where was Ephraim? His eighteen-year-old son was probably in the library. He was different from his older brother—studious and serious where Manasseh was playful and carefree. Well, it was only fair. The older son was like the mother, the younger son like the father.

Joseph rose from the cushioned chair where he had been watching the game and strolled into the library. There he found his son, reading a scroll.

Ephraim was a tall youth with a serious turn of mind. While his older brother preferred to play games with his mother, Ephraim buried himself in the ancient wisdom of Egypt. That was why, several years ago, Joseph had employed one of the leaders of Israel to come to his home and spend hours telling his sons the ancient stories of Israel.

They heard stories of the creation of the world, of the first people to live in the beautiful garden God had created, of their sin and disgrace, and of the great flood which had covered the earth. These stories, so carefully preserved in the oral tradition of his people, instilled deep respect for God, who not only created but rules the earth.

"Ephraim."

The young man looked up from his scroll. "Yes, Father?"

"This afternoon I am going to visit your grandfather in Goshen. Would you like to go?"

The youth smiled. "Of course, Father." Then his smile faded. "But I forgot. I must go to the home of Manelli today to study the hieroglyphics."

"Can you cancel?"

The boy shook his head. "I canceled last week, remember? Do you want me to forget everything I learned?"

Joseph chuckled. "No, my son. Your lessons from the scribe are important. You can visit Jacob another time."

He returned to the game room, where he found his mother and Manasseh finishing their game.

"She beat me," Manasseh grinned. "She always does."

Against the background of Asenath's delighted laugh,

Joseph said, "I'm not surprised. She may well be the best senit player in all Egypt."

Asenath came to Joseph, her face glowing. "I wish you'd play, dear. I'd like to beat you sometime."

Joseph took her hands. "I'm sure you could. Maybe that's why I don't play your silly games."

Joseph put his arm around his wife and led her outside into the garden. They strolled through the flowers and palm trees to the wall overlooking the Great River. Below them, the city of Hieropolis sat brooding in the sunlight.

"I'm going to Goshen this afternoon, my dear. Would you like to go?"

"Oh, yes!" She clapped her hand. "I'd love to see your father again. But only if we go by chair. I'll never ride in one of those horrid chariots again."

Joseph sighed. "All right. The chair it is. But you must spend time with Serah while I talk with my father."

Again the charming pout appeared on Asenath's face. Joseph smiled as he watched her lips purse, the eyebrows gather, and the nose twitch. This, to her husband at least, was one of her most endearing traits.

"All right," she said slowly. Then she brightened. "Maybe I can make her laugh again. I did that last time I saw her, remember?"

"I remember. When you told her about Manasseh catching the little alligator. Don't you two ever talk about anything serious?"

Asenath's laugh was soft. "With Serah, most of what we say is serious. She's so concerned about Jacob, that's about all she talks about. That's why I try to get her to laugh. She's a pretty girl when she smiles."

Serah was in her early twenties, but she practically lived at the home of her grandfather Jacob. She had assumed complete charge of the aging patriarch and tried to make him as comfortable as possible.

"Shall we take Manasseh?" asked Joseph.

"No." At the shake of Asenath's head, her little blue head cone almost upset. She had to hold it firmly on the top of her wig. "He is going for a chariot ride with Malekh today. You know he'd rather do that than take a slow chair ride with us to visit his grandfather."

Joseph nodded. His older son was as deeply involved in chariot riding as his younger son was in scholarship.

"Tell me, my dear." Joseph turned to Asenath and solemnly regarded her bright brown eyes. "How is it we can have two sons so different? I don't understand how they can be in the same family."

Asenath's cheeks dimpled as her puckish smile slowly spread over her face. "Why, that's easy, Joseph. One of them takes after you, the other after me."

He smiled tenderly. "Am I that serious?"

She nodded. "All the time. You hardly ever laugh. The only time you do is when I tell you to. And I'm telling you now. Laugh!"

Joseph laughed. "I guess," he said, "it's because I'm still a slave. Your slave. You have but to command, and I obey."

"And now I command you, come into the house. We must get ready to go to Goshen this afternoon."

Several hours later, Joseph sat with his father in the courtyard of Jacob's home. The house where the old man lived was larger and more comfortable than the other houses in Goshen. Joseph and his brothers felt that the patriarch of the clan should live in comparative luxury during his declining years.

Serah and Asenath were inside the house, and their conversation could faintly be heard. Joseph had yet to hear Serah laugh, although Asenath's bubbling laugh sounded often from within the building. It would only be a matter of time before the low-pitched laugh from the stern young woman would be heard.

"And how are you, Father?" Joseph asked. Asenath had asked the question only moments before, when she greeted her father-in-law. His answer had been cheerful. She had smiled and showered her optimism and gaiety on all corners of the house.

Jacob's answer to Joseph's question was quite different from his answer to the same question from Asenath.

"I am dying, my son."

Joseph accepted his answer gravely. "I know, Father. May you die in peace."

The old man sighed. "Peace comes from within, Joseph. I have found that."

Joseph looked thoughtfully at the patriarch. His long hair and beard, though combed and oiled, were stringy and sparse. The wrinkled face showed brown spots. the hands trembled. Yet the eyes were clear. Under shaggy white brows, they bored into Joseph's with fire and intelligence.

"How can I help you die, Father?"

The question sounded strange, but Joseph knew Jacob understood.

"I have one request, Joseph. You know what it is."

Joseph nodded. "It shall be done. I will arrange everything. Immediately after the mourning period following your death, we shall take your body to Canaan and bury you in the cave at Machpelah."

"Thank you, my son. That is all. No. I have another request."

"Tell me, Father."

The old man sucked for a moment on a tooth, one of the few remaining in his mouth. "Help my sons understand the Promise."

"I will, Father."

"Especially Judah. It is important for Judah to grasp the significance of the inheritance."

"Yes, Father."

"And Shiloh."

"Yes, Father. Shiloh."

The old man sighed. "Yes. Until Shiloh comes."

Old themes, discussed over and over until they had been reduced to monosyllables. Joseph stroked his chin. As often as they had discussed this, he still did not understand.

"Tell me again, Father. About Shiloh. Who is he? When will he come?"

The patriarch ran his fingers through his stringy white beard. "I don't know, Joseph. I don't know who he is or when he will come. I don't even know if Shiloh is a person. All I know is that one word. Shiloh."

Shiloh. One simple word. Literally, it meant "he to whom it belongs." But who was that?

"Tell me, Father, why is that one word so important? Did God speak to you?"

Jacob gazed into space above Joseph's head. He was silent for a moment. At last he spoke, his voice soft.

"Yes, God did, my son. How, I just don't know. There are so many things I don't know. It seems the older I get, the less I know. Why is it that when we are young, we know so much? Now, as we grow old, we know so little."

Jacob's eyes returned to Joseph's face. "I don't know how God spoke to me. When I was young, God spoke in a dream. As I grew older, God spoke to me through a man I wrestled with at the ford of the Jabbok River. Now—now God still speaks to me, but I just don't know how."

He shook his head slowly. "Maybe after I die, I'll find out some of the answers to these mysteries. Maybe then God will speak to me, and explain all these dark secrets."

"But Father, how can I explain Shiloh to Judah and the others if you can't explain it fully to me?"

Jacob sighed. "Do the best you can, my son. Some day,

the vision will be made clear. Until then, just hold on to it. Tightly. Never let it go. Never. Until Shiloh comes."

Joseph nodded. "I will, Father. I promise."

"And what are you promising now, Joseph?"

Asenath's cheerful voice reached him from the doorway of the house. Joseph turned to see the two women standing there. He noted the contrast. Asenath, the complete Egyptian lady, wearing a bright blue kalasaris, the greasecone on her head already causing her face to shine. Serah, the Israelite, wore a plain woolen dress, bound at the waist by a leather girdle, her smooth black hair combed and oiled. One smiled, the other looked stern.

"We must go, Joseph," said Asenath. "I want to be home before dark."

Behind her, Serah glared at Joseph. She would not say anything inflammatory in the presence of her tiring grandfather, but her eyes flashed defiance. Joseph was disturbing the rest of her beloved patient.

Joseph rose. "Serah, please call for our chair. We shall leave at once."

Serah left, a look of relief on her face, and headed toward the back of the house where the slaves were waiting.

Asenath hurried over to Jacob and placed her hand on his. "I hope we didn't tire you too much, Father Israel."

Jacob smiled. "It was good to see you again, my child. Even if you didn't make Serah laugh."

The slaves who carried the chair into the courtyard were surprised to find their great master and his lovely wife laughing so heartily. The laughter was infectious, and they too smiled.

Only Serah frowned. She wished they would leave. Her grandfather was sick. He was an old man; couldn't they see that? He needed his rest. What did they have to talk about that was so important, anyway?

20

"Father!"

Ephraim called from another room. In a moment he burst in, still clutching a papyrus scroll. "There's a messenger here from Goshen. He ran all the way."

Joseph sprang to his feet, instantly concerned. Two months had passed since his last visit to Goshen. Jacob was much older than the average Egyptian, who was considered extremely old if he lived to be sixty. In fact, Joseph himself was considered a very old man in Egypt.

The messenger was Bela, Benjamin's firstborn son. Benjamin was well on his way to fulfilling Pharaoh Sutekh's benediction several years ago, when he predicted Jacob's youngest boy would have many sons. He had nine, and the tenth was expected in a few months.

Bela was out of breath from his run. Ephraim had said he ran all the way, and it was several miles from Goshen to Hieropolis. Yes, his message would be urgent.

"Greetings, Uncle Joseph," he panted. "I have been sent to tell you—Grandfather Israel . . . is dying!"

The news was not unexpected. Yet when it came, it shocked Joseph. They had become close. A mutual love and respect had grown between them. They had probed each others' minds and souls, and their discussions went beyond anything Joseph's brothers could comprehend or were even interested in.

Now the old man was dying. Joseph would go at once. His sons should go too. Quickly he gave orders for two chariots to be made ready. It would only take about an hour by chariot.

Asenath loved Jacob and wanted to go but knew she must stay. This was men's business. The dying patriarch would want to give his sons a final blessing. It was proper for a woman to visit a sick old man but not to be present at his death.

Manasseh mounted one chariot and took the reins from the professional driver. The young man's high spirits were infectious, and the driver stood aside with a smile. The boy Bela stepped in beside him. The three-man chariot had enough space for the boy, the youth, and the driver.

In the other chariot, Joseph and Ephraim mounted and stood behind the professional driver. Ephraim was not as adventurous as his older brother, and driving a chariot on a wild ride to Goshen did not appeal to him. And so on the road to Goshen, laughter and shouts came from one chariot, silence and solemnity from the other.

As they drove down the valley road, they saw large flocks of sheep grazing on the green hillsides. In the deeper valleys, the herds of cattle roamed the pastures. The land had been good to the family of Israel. After only eighteen years, they were prospering and growing.

Small houses appeared as they plunged deeper into the valley. They were permanent houses made of bricks, much more substantial than the tents they had occupied back in Canaan. The people had prospered too, not only in livestock but in their gardens. They had plenty to eat.

As the two chariots rattled into the yard, Joseph could see that every effort had been made to show respect for the dying patriarch.

The yard outside the house was full of people. Joseph's brothers were all there, along with many of their sons. The death of the clan's patriarch was a momentous occasion. Joseph and his sons pressed through the crowd into the house, accepting solemn greetings as they went.

Jacob lay on a couch attended by Asher's daughter Serah. She had ordered everyone out of the house and had completely taken over the care of her dying grandfather. Joseph shared Asenath's views about his niece Serah and her domineering qualities. She was accepted and tolerated because she was exactly what Jacob needed in his last year.

Serah had married a Canaanite nobody liked. She had been forced to take over control of her own family until her husband's death, when she had moved in with her grandfather Jacob. Now her domineering ways were felt by every man and woman in the clan.

"He's sleeping, Joseph."

Serah had no awe for the former Grain Administrator of Egypt. To her he was just another intruder.

"I am not asleep, child!" Jacob's voice was strong despite his weakened condition. "Help me sit. I want to talk to my son Joseph."

Serah glowered at both men, not only at being called a child, but also because her sick-room rule had been challenged. But Jacob was the patriarch of the clan. She must obey. She made the old man as comfortable as possible and stood protectively by his side.

"Now get out!" Jacob muttered testily. Serah sniffed, but left the room, shaking her head and muttering.

"How are you, Father?" asked Joseph tenderly.

"I am dying."

These were the same words he always used in response to Joseph's question. There was no hesitation in this bold statement, nor regret. He simply stated a fact.

"That is so, Father." Joseph knew better than to try to deceive the shrewd old man on the couch. Too much honesty had passed between them over the years for that.

"God is good." The old man raised his white eyebrows and looked at his son. "God has kept his promises. He has made my children into a mighty nation, as he said he would. Now, where are your sons?"

"Here, Father."

The two boys stepped forward. They were awed in the presence of the venerable old man on his deathbed.

"Joseph, I'm going to adopt them as my own."

Joseph gasped. His sons did not know what this meant, but he did. It meant they would receive an equal portion of the inheritance with all the other sons of Jacob. Already the nation of Israel had begun to subdivide into tribes. Manasseh and Ephraim would claim an equal part with Reuben and Judah and all the others.

"But why, Father?"

"Because of your mother, Rachel, whom I buried near Ephrath."

Joseph nodded. There was more, much more, but Jacob did not have the strength to go into detail.

Joseph's mother had named him Joseph, meaning "another." She had wanted more children. But only one more child had been born: Benjamin, and that child's birth had caused his mother's death.

Now Rachel had two more sons—Manasseh and Ephraim. Their adoption was a symbolic gesture perhaps, but very meaningful to Jacob. And to Joseph also.

"Joseph." The old man on the bed seemed to be gathering his strength. "Place the boys on my knees."

Joseph knew what that meant. When a baby was born, he was placed on the knees of his father or mother. The child was acknowledged and given his name. In this case, it meant Jacob would formally adopt these two boys and give them the inheritance blessing.

The two young men were much too old to be placed on Jacob's knees, but Joseph instructed his sons to kneel beside the bed and place their hands on the bony knees. He made sure Manasseh knelt on Jacob's right and Ephraim on the left, with their hands in place.

Jacob's hands went to their heads. "Are these the boys?" he asked. He could not see well.

"They are, Father. Manasseh the firstborn is on your right, and Ephraim on your left."

Something in Jacob's mind reacted to Joseph's statement. His hands dropped to the bed, then lifted again. This time he crossed his arms, and placed his right hand on Ephraim's head and his left on Manasseh's.

"May God, the God of our fathers Abraham and Isaac, who has been by shepherd all my life, bless these two boys. May God watch over them and keep them from harm, as he has done for me in my life. May these boys be a blessing to my name and to our ancestors Abraham and Isaac, and may they be fathers of mighty nations!"

It was done. Joseph frowned and stroked his chin. His father had given the older son's blessing to Ephraim and the younger son's blessing to Manasseh.

"Why, Father? Why did you give the birthright blessing to my younger son?"

Jacob's hands dropped weakly to the bed. "I know what I'm doing, my son." He closed his eyes for a minute, then opened them and squinted up at Joseph. "Don't worry. It's not the birthright blessing containing the Promise. Both boys will be equally blessed. May all my sons be as prosperous as Ephraim and Manasseh!"

Joseph accepted the inevitable. It was done, and he couldn't change it. It wasn't that important, anyway. And he thought he understood. He recognized a trace of the old Jacob still in Israel, a relic of the old perversity which had plagued him all his life.

The younger son claiming the birthright. Jacob had done that himself in his youth, when he had cheated his brother out of the elder son's right to inherit. And he had even displaced his oldest son Reuben, and installed Judah in the birthright position. And now he had done it with Ephraim and Manasseh.

Ephraim and Manasseh. He would have to get used to calling them in their new order. Maybe it was just as well. The studious, serious young man would come first, his frivolous older brother second. Jacob might be dying, but his wits hadn't left him yet.

Jacob lay quietly on the bed, his eyes closed. Joseph softly told his sons they could leave now. The young men only dimly understood what had happened. They knew they had been adopted by Israel, but the full significance of this act escaped them. Some day they would know. Some day they would recall this moment, and know what the old man on his deathbed had done for them.

Joseph sat at his father's bedside for several minutes. Jacob seemed to be asleep, perhaps gathering strength. Eventually Joseph opened his eyes.

"Joseph."

"I'm here, Father."

"Now send in my sons. I will bless them."

"Yes, Father."

"And Joseph." He chuckled. "Don't let that shrew Serah come back to fuss over me. I only have one chance to die. I'd like to do it without her!"

21

Joseph joined the others outside the house. The chilly night had sneaked up on them and banished the warm day. Joseph shivered.

Suddenly Serah was there. She draped a woolen cape around his shoulders. She had done the same for his sons, he noticed. Domineering she might be, but also thoughtful and motherly. No wonder the family tolerated her.

Joseph called his brothers to gather with him at Jacob's bedside. They shifted uneasily as Jacob said, "Now it is time for me to give each of you my last words. Reuben, you first. Everyone else wait outside."

Reuben came out soon, scowling and red faced. He would say nothing about what his father had told him. Simeon followed, then Levi. Their reaction was the same.

When Judah came out, he wore a puzzled frown. He called Joseph to him. "Walk with me, brother."

When they were far enough down the road that no one could hear, Judah turned to Joseph. "I'm confused."

"Tell me, Judah."

"He said—" Judah paused. "Well, at first he said my brothers would praise me and bow before me. I understand that. I am already leader of our clan."

He paused again, trying to recall the exact words. "He said, 'The scepter shall not depart from Judah until Shiloh comes.' I don't understand."

Joseph nodded. Shiloh again. His father's favorite word. A word whose mystery Jacob seemed to relish.

"He to whom it belongs." Joseph spoke slowly, trying to fathom the depths of the words' meaning. Joseph struggled to explain what he only vaguely understood.

"Father has spoken to me about this before," he said. "He has honored you above all of us. Not only do you lead our clan; you have inherited the birthright. That is at least part of the meaning of Shiloh."

"The birthright?" Judah wrinkled his forehead and stroked his beard. "What does birthright mean, the way the clan is now? There are twelve of us. We each have an equal inheritance. Of what value is the birthright now?"

Joseph made a mental note to explain later that there were no longer twelve of them, but thirteen—not counting himself, since his two sons would inherit his share. Judah had not heard about Jacob's adoption of Ephraim and Manasseh. Now, however, Joseph must explain Shiloh.

"In our family, the birthright has a special significance. It's not a matter of material inheritance, but rather of something intangible being passed down. God has chosen our clan for a special destiny. God gave our ancestor Abraham a Promise, and God has repeated this Promise to both Isaac and Israel. The Promise is that through our clan, God's hand will touch all people of the world."

Joseph paused. Judah looked at him hopefully, his mind open to further explanation. He already knew what Joseph had said so far; it was part of the tradition of the family.

Joseph continued. "We are becoming a great nation, which is part of God's Promise. But our father believes—no, God has told him—that there will be a special line, running through the generations of our descendants. The line will pass down, generation after generation, until Shiloh comes. This Shiloh will receive the scepter from his predecessors, then be a blessing to all the people of the world."

"God told him this?"

"So he says."

"But . . . just who is Shiloh ?"

Joseph shrugged. "Who knows? A king, or a whole dynasty of kings. Maybe one special king. I don't know."

Judah sighed. "And this—this Shiloh will come through my descendants. But how does our father know that?"

Again Joseph shrugged. "He was closer to God than any of us. Maybe he knows things about the future we don't."

"Hmmm." Judah frowned. "Shiloh. 'He to whom the scepter will come.' One person. Incredible!"

"Maybe it isn't one person." Joseph felt he had to be honest with Judah. "It may refer to our whole nation—the people of Israel. Or maybe only one tribe is Shiloh."

Judah sighed. "We're talking about a future we can't know, Joseph. We can only live in the present."

"That's wise." Joseph's heart went out to his practical brother, for whom philosophical discussions were hard.

"But remember Father's words, Judah. Mark them well in your heart. Pass them on to your descendants. They must never be forgotten."

The brothers turned and walked slowly back along the road toward Jacob's house. Joseph sighed. He felt strongly the presence of the dying man. A giant was falling! Not since Abraham had a man lived who was closer to God.

Why did inspiration seem to skip a generation? God spoke to Abraham, then skipped Isaac. But then came Israel, the man who wrestled with God. And after Jacob? There were Reuben and Judah and the others, including himself. Practical, down-to-earth men, not mystical saints who walked with God. They had nothing of God's word but the tradition passed down to them. So be it. They must pass on the tradition faithfully, until another saint came.

Or until Shiloh came?

Why didn't God speak to all of them, as he had to Abraham and Israel? Why hadn't God spoken to Joseph? But maybe God had, in God's own way. Joseph always knew God was with him, not because he spoke to him in words, but because of the things that happened. Only God could have made them happen.

Yes. God had spoken to him. Not in words, but in the events of his life. He could see that now. And this voice of God was just as real as if God had spoken orally.

Judah had been as silent as Joseph. Perhaps he was as absorbed in his thoughts as Joseph was in his. In the house, Joseph found Jacob prostrate, eyes closed, body visibly exhausted by the ordeal of blessing his sons. Joseph knelt by the bed, and felt his father's hand on his head.

"Joseph? My favorite son?"

"I'm here, Father."

Jacob opened his eyes, and the fever of inspiration still burned in them. His voice was weak, but the words tumbled out almost mechanically.

"Joseph is a tender vine growing along the wall. Well watered. Bearing fruit. His enemies tried to cut him down, but he was protected. His protector was God. May God continue to bless and protect him. Almighty God of our fathers, bless him from heaven above and earth beneath.

"Blessing of the hills and valleys; blessing of the womb and breasts; blessings of eternity. May these blessings fall on Joseph, my favorite, who is different from his brothers!"

The hand fell away, and Jacob closed his feverish eyes. He breathed deeply. Joseph thought he was sleeping.

Joseph was profoundly moved. His father was under deep inspiration. He went over the words in his mind and determined to study them in the years ahead. They were momentous words. He hoped his brothers would remember all Jacob had said and preserve the words for posterity.

His first impression of his blessing was that it spoke only of the present, not the future. Ephraim and Manasseh had received blessings predicting their future and that of their descendants. So had Judah, and probably all the others. But Joseph's blessing was only for himself, not his descendants. He frowned briefly. That was because he had no descendants, since his sons had been adopted by Jacob. There would never be a tribe of Joseph.

No tribe of Joseph. Even though he was the favorite, he would have no inheritance. And a son of Leah would be the heir of the Promise.

Was it too late to change that? Did his father have enough life in him to be persuaded to at least insure that the line of Shiloh would come through Ephraim? No. The old patriarch was too far gone. Let him die in peace.

He glanced down at the old man on the bed. Israel clung to life by a tenuous thread. The blessings had wrung from him the remaining reserves of strength. His breath now came in gasps, and the rattle in his throat meant he had only moments left.

Jacob opened his mouth to speak again and with one last burst of strength he said, "Now call all my sons to gather again around me."

With Joseph at his head and the others close by, Jacob whispered, "Bury me . . . at Machpelah . . . where I buried Leah."

Joseph thought these were Jacob's last words, but they weren't. One more came gasping out as Jacob looked directly at Joseph.

"Shalom."

There was one final intake of breath, one final rattle in the throat. The brothers bowed their heads. Joseph wept.

But he didn't weep long. His active mind fastened on his father's last word. *"Shalom."* The word for "peace." It was used as a greeting or farewell, a benediction wishing peace upon the person spoken to. Jacob's last word to his favorite son was appropriate.

Then suddenly Joseph straightened, his sorrow forgotten. His father's last word loomed large in his mind. *Shalom.* This was Israel, who wrestled with God. His life had been a never-ceasing struggle with God, and through much hardship and trial he had been striving with his deeper faith, continually wrestling with the man of the Jabbok River. Strife and turmoil and conflict. All his life.

And his dying word was "peace." *Joseph is a tender vine, growing along the wall.* His father's blessing to him. So beautiful. So incisive. He had heard that a dying man's words were sometimes his greatest. And the blessing to his favorite son certainly bore that out.

Favorite son, indeed!

May these blessings fall on Joseph, my favorite, who is different from his brothers!

Yes, he was different. He would have no inheritance. No posterity. No descendants to remember him. And the Promise—the Promise would be fulfilled through Judah, a son of Leah.

Leah, the matriarch of Israel. Buried in the cave at Machpelah, awaiting Jacob's body to lie beside her. One of her sons would receive Israel's richest inheritance.

Yet his father must have retained some of the old affection for his mother, Rachel. The only way he could have shown her honor would be to increase her children from two to four. He had done that when he had adopted Ephraim and Manasseh.

But in doing so, he had disinherited his favorite son. Now Joseph had no children. And no Promise.

Joseph shrugged. He would have to accept it. It was God's will. Long ago, shortly after being sold into slavery, Joseph had accepted mediocrity as his lot in life. Success and high office had been thrust upon him, but he had never reached for it. In the eyes of Egypt, he had attained a height that was almost as lofty as the Pharaoh himself.

But he was an Israelite, not an Egyptian. No matter how many honors and fame had come his way in Egypt, he was still a son of Israel. And proud to be just that.

But in Israel—in Israel he was nobody. And never would be. History would remember Ephraim and Manasseh, but not Joseph.

So be it. He bowed his head in acceptance. Success and a place in history in Egypt, but mediocrity and anonymity in the history of Israel. And by the time Shiloh comes, nobody would remember Joseph.

Strange, so strange, are the ways of Israel's God.

The Author

James R. Shott took early retirement from the Presbyterian ministry in 1980 to pursue a new career as a freelance writer. He has had many short stories, articles, and poems published in various magazines, but he thinks of himself as a writer of novels.

His first book, *The House Across the Street*, was a children's book published by Winston-Derek Publishers in 1988. *Leah*, a biblical novel, was published by Herald Press in 1990. The Old Testament period of the patriarchs claims his major interest. He is at work on other novels about this era.

An ordained Presbyterian minister, Shott holds degrees from Westminster College (New Wilmington, Pa.) and Pittsburgh Theological Seminary. A native of western Pennsylvania, he now lives in Palm Bay, Florida.

Shott attends the First Presbyterian Church in Palm Bay. He is a devoted family man, and he and his wife, Esther, spend as much time as possible with their seven grandchildren.